Joan Lingard

The Stolen Sister

Catnip

CATNIP BOOKS
Published by Catnip Publishing Ltd.
14 Greville Street
London
EC1N 8SB

This edition first published 2011

1 3 5 7 9 10 8 6 4 2

Text copyright © Joan Lingard, 2011
The moral right of the author has been asserted.

A CIP catalogue record for this book is available from the British Library.

ISBN 978-1-84647-1292

Printed in Poland

www.catnippublishing.co.uk

For Catriona and Angie

Eilidh and Mhairi

and Joe

Contents

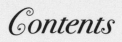

Chapter One:
A Kidnapping

The day began as usual at the *Pig and Whistle* with no hint of what was to come. Elfie and Ivy had their regular squabble over a hairbrush and Joe was first down for breakfast, wearing his black suit and white shirt with its stand-up, starched collar.

By the time Elfie arrived in the kitchen, Ma Bigsby, canvas apron wrapped around her stout body, was stirring porridge in the big black pot and the other ten orphans were seated at the table. Not that they considered themselves to be orphans now. Ma and Pa Bigsby had become their parents. They were waiting for Pa now.

When he entered the kitchen he was dressed, as always, in a lilac-coloured suit, his white, flowing hair neatly brushed.

'Good morning, children,' he greeted them.

'Good morning, Pa,' they chorused.

He seated himself and unrolled his napkin. Mabel, the eldest of the children at fifteen, passed around the bowls of porridge, aided by Ivy, who managed to slop a little of Elfie's on the table.

'Look what's she done!' cried Elfie.

'Now don't start,' warned Ma. 'You're twelve, the two of you. Not babies any longer.'

Elfie glowered but subsided.

Pa said Grace and they began to eat.

'Anything special on today, Joe?' asked Pa.

'Not as far as I know.' Joe's voice was sombre. 'We badly need more clients.'

He worked for Elfie's lawyer father, Alfred Trelawney, now that he was fourteen years old and had finished school. Trelawney had fallen on hard times and been forced to move from his elegant chambers in Chancery Lane to a rather shabby office in Holborn.

'It takes time to build up a business again,' said Pa.

'I sometimes think I'm more of a hindrance than a help to him.'

'Don't talk rubbish, Joe!' cried Elfie. 'Papa says he doesn't know what he'd do without you. He says you'll make a brilliant lawyer.'

'It's not that.' Joe shook his head. 'Some people are put off by the sight of me, you know that.'

'They must be stupid people.'

'Unenlightened,' agreed Pa. 'And, sadly, there are too many of them around. But you cannot bow to them, Joe.'

'Anyway, most of it was Clarissa's fault, that Papa went bankrupt.' Elfie was heating up again. 'Poor old Clarissa! She sits there mumping and moaning about coming down in the world, having to give up her big house in Hampstead and her carriage and her servants . . .'

'Eat up your porridge,' said Ma. 'And that's no way to talk about your father's wife. She's your stepmother.'

Elfie snorted. She had never known her own mother but she was sure she would not have been anything like Clarissa Trelawney. 'If she hadn't run up all them bills, Papa wouldn't have had so many debts.'

'*Those* bills,' murmured Joe, giving her a grin. He and Pa Bigsby loved to pick up other people's mistakes in grammar. Not Ma's, though. She could say anything she liked and get away with it.

'What you say is true, Elfie. In part, at least.' Pa dabbed his lips with his snow-white napkin when he had finished eating. He was very fastidious in his habits. 'But your father's former partner must take some of the blame.'

Pa gave Elfie a smile. That man, Basildon-Blunt he had called himself, was now behind bars. It was Joe and Elfie who had helped to put him there.

Joe was eyeing the wall clock. 'I'd better be going.'

'I'll come with you to the bus stop.' Elfie sprang up.

'But you are *not* to be get on the bus, Elfie,' warned Pa. 'Not even for one stop!'

'Bet she will,' put in Ivy.

Elfie longed to slap her but that kind of thing was not put up with at the *Pig and Whistle*. When she'd lived rough with other street kids she'd often had to fight for her life. But not here. Ma and Pa believed in 'civilised' behaviour.

'We shall be starting lessons in ten minutes,' Pa announced. 'Your algebra is sadly in need of attention, Elfie. And don't make a face either!'

'Please may I leave the table?'

'You already seem to have done,' observed Ma. 'And what do you say?'

'Thank you for breakfast,' gabbled Elfie.

'Ten minutes,' repeated Pa.

Elfie followed Joe out into the street. He had picked up his black bowler from the hall table and was carrying it under his arm. He hated wearing the hat, just as he did the starched collar, and would put it on only when he got off the bus at the other end.

They joined the queue at the stop.

'Is Papa very worried?' asked Elfie.

Joe sighed. 'Money's so tight we might have to find another office.'

'Again?'

'We could get a cheaper place at King's Cross. Trouble then is you only get a certain kind of client.'

'Ones with no money?'

Joe nodded. 'We've got some of those already. And your papa's soft-hearted. He doesn't turn anyone away.'

'You wouldn't either, would you?'

'Probably not.'

'He could save money if he'd let Rosalind come to Pa Bigsby's school. It's free.' Elfie's half-sister was still attending her old school where they had to pay fees.

'You know her mother would never let her.'

Clarissa had said she was prepared to make sacrifices herself but not to ask them of Rosalind.

'Clarissa might just have to change her mind!' Elfie tossed her head. 'Anyway, Rosalind *wants* to come. She loves the *Pig and Whistle*. There's far more going on here than on her own in that big house with only the maid for company. And there's no better teacher in the whole of London than Pa Bigsby.'

They were both agreed about that.

Elfie leant out from the bus stop and peered along the street. It was busy with the morning rush. Carts rattled along in amongst the more sedate cabs and carriages. There was even the occasional motor car. Elfie's dad had owned one for a while but he had to sell it – they were so expensive to run.

'Here it comes, Joe! The good old number 49.'

The dark green bus came swaying into the stop behind its three strong horses.

'Whoa!' cried the driver, bringing the horses to a halt. They stood, snorting a little, their flanks quivering and shiny with sweat, while the queue surged forward. Elfie was tempted. She wished she could go with Joe. She loved riding the buses.

But she stopped herself just in time. Pa Bigsby would

not be pleased if she was late for school. 'I'll come to the office this afternoon after I've finished my chores.'

'See you then!' Joe leapt aboard.

Elfie waved until the bus was out of sight. Lucky Joe. The 49 would take him to Islington where he would change onto the number 89 for Holborn Viaduct. Elfie knew all about the bus routes and which number went where in London.

She turned reluctantly and with slow steps made her way back inside to the schoolroom and to algebra. Who on earth had ever thought that one up!

$$\infty$$

In the afternoon the older children did various chores to earn money for the household. It cost a lot to feed thirteen mouths and the pub was not frequented by toffs who spent bags of money. One of their regulars, Mad Meg, sister of Sad Sid, only ever asked for a glass of water. Ma Bigsby didn't mind. Often she'd give Mad Meg a glass of barley water on the house.

A good few of the *Pig and Whistle* customers had come across the sea from Ireland, like Ma herself. There were a lot of Irish people in North London but some pubs didn't encourage them and a number of letting houses even had notices in their windows saying: 'No Irish. No Jews.' Pa Bigsby made it quite clear that he disapproved of such discrimination.

Often, Elfie's chore was to help Billy with deliveries around Stoke Newington. She liked that, being out and about and meeting different people. Mabel and Ivy went to an establishment run by a Miss Swanston to sew lace on pillowcases and nightgowns. They said it was more ladylike than humping parcels and Miss Swanston gave them a piece of Turkish Delight if they worked hard. Elfie told them they were welcome to it! She hated the stuff. All gooey and sticky. Give her a black-and-white striped ball to suck any day. She loved their minty flavour. Next year, when Billy turned 14, he hoped to start work on the railway. He was mad about trains. Elfie hoped she could carry on doing his deliveries.

That afternoon they were working for Mr Huckleberry, the ironmonger, whose parcels tended to be heavy. They trundled the loaded barrows through the streets as fast as they could, weaving in and out of the pedestrians, raising an odd curse here and there if they came too close to tripping them up. Both Elfie and Billy had a reason for wanting to finish early.

As soon as the last parcel had been delivered and the barrows returned to the shop they took to their heels. They raced back to Green Lanes, to the corner where they waited for lifts. They were in luck today. A carter they knew came along within five minutes, carrying a load of timber. He waved to them and pulled into the side straightaway. They clambered onto the back and clung onto the sides as he set off again.

When they reached King's Cross, Billy jumped off.

'Ta, Tommy,' he cried and dived into the station.

Tommy turned round to talk to Elfie. 'I'm goin' along towards Holborn,' he said . 'Any use to you?'

She nodded. This really must be her lucky day!

'Hang on then, Elf!'

Tommy was in quite a hurry. She almost got tipped off at the next corner and had a few scratches by the time they made it to Holborn, but it was worth it to get a free ride. She thanked Tommy, hopped down, and ran along the street towards her father's office.

Alfred Trelawney's previous chambers in Chancery Lane had sported a large gleaming brass plate on the front door and several comfortably furnished rooms on the ground floor. Things were different now. The nameplate here was small and the premises, which were were two floors up a dark stair, consisted of a tiny waiting room, an office where both her father and Joe worked, a lavatory with a wash-hand basin, and a cupboard. To begin with some of their old clients had continued to come, but as time went on fewer of them made the extra journey. Elfie decided they probably hadn't liked climbing the stairs for a start.

There were no clients waiting today. Elfie tapped briefly on the office door and put her head round.

'Come in, love.'

Her dad rose from his seat and came to give her a hug. Joe smiled at her.

'Anyone been in?' she asked.

'A docker,' Joe answered. 'His friend was nicked for stealing a bottle of rum. Swears he's innocent. Wanted to know if we could help him. We couldn't.'

A lot of petty thieving went on at the docks. When Elfie had been homeless she'd hung around that area regularly. She felt sorry for the dockers. They worked hard and didn't earn much.

'We'll have to do something,' Elfie declared, 'to bring more clients in.'

'We can hardly drag people in off the street, dear,' said her father.

Elfie wasn't so sure about that.

'Why don't we make some leaflets?' suggested Joe. 'It'd be a way to advertise the firm.'

'We could go round and put them through the doors of posh houses,' added Elfie.

'Trouble is I haven't got a posh office.' Her father sighed. 'It's one of my problems. People with money like to think you're successful.'

Elfie got up and went to the window. How could they just sit there waiting? She gazed glumly down into the street and watched a lady climbing out of a cab. Her face was shielded from the sunshine by her wide straw hat. The cabbie handed her down and then climbed back to his perch. The lady seemed to be coming towards their downstairs' door. Maybe, just maybe, it was a client. Elfie squinted but couldn't make out any more. The hat had moved out of sight.

Joe cocked his head. 'Sounds like someone's coming up the stairs.'

They listened. There definitely were footsteps on the

stairs. They grew louder and louder, and seemed to speed up as they got closer.

'Sounds as if they're in a hurry,' observed Joe.

'Maybe desperate for help,' said Elfie hopefully and went to open the door.

She peered down into the stairwell. The woman she'd seen in the street had stopped and was gasping for breath. In her hand she held the straw hat. She gazed up at Elfie, her wide blue eyes anxious and fearful.

'Cor luv' a duck,' cried Elfie, resorting to one of Ma Bigsby's favourite sayings. 'If it ain't Rosalind's mum!'

Her father jumped out of his chair and went dashing down the stairs.

'What's wrong, Clarissa? Are you all right?'

Clarissa was trying to speak. 'Rosalind . . .' She couldn't go on. Elfie could see that she was out of breath, but she was also on the verge of tears. Clarissa sat down suddenly in the stairwell and let go of the straw hat, which went floating down into the murky depths of the stairwell.

'What's happened to Rosalind?' Alfred Trelawney put his arm round his wife's trembling shoulders.

'She's . . .' Clarissa gulped.

'She's *what*? Tell me, Clarissa!'

'She's disappeared,'

'How can she *disappear*?'

'Alfred, I think she's been kidnapped!'

Chapter Two:
Looking for Rosalind

'Fetch her a drink of water, Joe,' cried Elfie, as she and her father helped Clarissa up the last few stairs. 'Quickly!'

Clarissa felt limp, as if she had no bones in her body and her face was chalky-white.

They managed to ease her into a chair. Unfortunately there were no cushions around to prop behind her head. She was trembling from head to foot by this time. Elfie's father stood behind her, cradling her shoulders, speaking softly.

'It's all right now, Clarissa,' he kept saying. 'Everything is going to be all right. There must be some mistake.'

Gradually Clarissa began to breathe a little more easily and a spot of colour returned to her cheeks.

Joe returned with a thick white mug. He held it out to her and after a slight hesitation she took it into her hand. Clarissa Trelawney was more familiar with the finest bone china. For a second Joe's finger touched hers and Elfie couldn't help noticing that she winced. Immediately, Elfie wanted to scream at her stepmother's reaction to her best friend, but this was not the moment. She knew why Clarissa had winced. She hadn't liked her soft white hand being touched by a black one.

'Now then, Clarissa,' said Alfred Trelawney gently, once his wife's breathing had returned to normal. 'What is all this about?'

'Rosalind's disappeared.' She spoke dully now. She was exhausted.

'How on earth could she *disappear*? Did she not come home from school as normal?'

Clarissa shook her head.

'You mean she didn't come home? *At all*?'

'No, not at all.'

'Was she invited to a friend's house? For tea perhaps? She sometimes is.'

Clarissa shook her head again.

'Did you not send a cab for her as usual?'

'Yes.'

'Well?'

'The cabbie came back to say she had already been collected.'

'How could that be?'

'Maybe she's been kidnapped?' suggested Elfie.

'Of course she's not been kidnapped.' Her father spoke sharply.

Elfie was worried. There *were* people who took children. Elfie herself had once been inveigled into a house by a couple who had wanted her to be their daughter. She had escaped by climbing out of the bedroom window. Rosalind was never allowed to go out on her own and she wouldn't be any good at climbing out of top-floor windows. Elfie decided that it wouldn't be helpful to point that out, however. Her father was looking fraught.

'But, Clarissa,' he went on, 'you know that Rosalind's school doesn't release any of the children until they are collected by someone responsible. Or unless a cab or a carriage is sent with a note of permission from a parent.'

'A cab did come with a note, so they let her go.' Clarissa started to weep. 'The note had my signature on it.'

'That's impossible!'

'The caretaker assures me it was signed,' she sobbed.

'Anyone can forge a signature,' put in Joe. 'I presume the cabbie kept the note?'

'It seems so.'

'There must be some confusion.' Alfred Trelawney got up. 'I shall telephone the school.'

'I have done,' said Clarissa. 'An hour ago.'

But her husband was already lifting the receiver and mouthpiece from their hook. He waited while the operator put him through to the school.

'May I speak to the headmistress, if you please? Yes, Miss Thorpe.'

'She wasn't any help,' moaned Clarissa. 'I told you, Alfred.'

But he was listening intently, his forehead creased with the worry of it all.

'Are you absolutely sure, Miss Thorpe?' he said, finally. 'That the cab driver definitely had a note signed by my wife?' There was a pause. 'But she had not signed it!'

'Of course I didn't!' cried Clarissa.

'I accept what you say, Miss Thorpe.' Alfred Trelawney was doing his best to stay calm. 'I am not in any way trying to lay blame on the school. But can you please give me the names, addresses and telephone numbers of any of my daughter's friends? Yes, I appreciate that you do not like to give out confidential information but this is serious and my wife's address book is at home. You must appreciate that we need to act quickly.' He was almost shouting by now, ruffling his free hand through his thick dark curly hair. Hair just like Elfie's. 'My daughter is *missing*, Miss Thorpe, do you understand? We shall have to call the police. Very well.' He turned to Joe. 'Have you got a pad and a pen? She's going to give me a couple of names.'

He repeated the names of two girls – Henrietta White and Mary Chesterton-Jones – with their details, as Miss Thorpe dictated them. Joe made notes in his neat square handwriting.

'Thank you, Miss Thorpe. Yes, yes, of course I will let you know.'

Alfred Trelawney's face was ashen as he turned towards them. 'There *has* to be some mistake. The cab must have come for some other girl. The caretaker has got confused. He never did strike me as being a very bright fellow.'

'Papa,' said Elfie, 'Rosalind might have gone to the *Pig*. That time before when she ran away she came there. Remember?'

'So she did.' His voice perked up. Little Rosalind had walked all the way to Stoke Newington in the middle of the night. It took her hours but she had been safe.

'Ring the Bigsbys then!' begged Clarissa.

'We don't have a telephone at the *Pig*,' Elfie pointed out.

'No *telephone*?'

'We don't need one,' said Joe.

'Most people we know don't have telephones,' added Elfie.

'Let us go to the *Pig and Whistle* at once.' Alfred Trelawney lifted his jacket from the back of his chair. 'Could you go down and see if you can find us a cab please, Joe?'

Joe went ahead with Elfie at his heels. Her father followed more slowly, supporting his wife.

Joe spotted a cab straightaway and raised his arm. The cab did stop but the cabbie eyed Joe and Elfie with suspicion until he saw Alfred Trelawney emerging from the building. He then jumped down from his perch and helped Clarissa to board. There was room for four in the back, two on each side.

Alfred Trelawney told the cabbie they had no time to waste.

'Very well, sir,' responded the cabbie. 'Hold tight then!'

He cracked his whip and they were off. They had a rocky ride through the busy London streets, swaying from side to side, holding on as advised. Horns blared around them and Clarissa emitted small screams from time to time and cried out on one particularly bad corner that they were all going to be killed.

Joe and Elfie sprang out the moment they came to rest outside the *Pig and Whistle*. Elfie ran on inside. Florrie, their barmaid, was behind the counter cleaning the brasses, getting ready to open up. She always looked so stylish. Today she was wearing a pink satin blouse with a high collar and leg of mutton sleeves and her long pearl earrings were birling as usual as she worked.

'You're in a hurry, young Elfie,' she called.

Elfie was still gasping for breath after the hectic ride. 'Have you seen Rosalind?'

'Rosalind?' repeated Florrie. 'Your little sister? Today, do you mean? *Here?*'

'Yes, yes . . . have you?'

'No. What's up?'

Elfie didn't even pause to answer, but made straight for the kitchen. Ma Bigsby was at the stove and Mabel was setting out plates on the table.

Elfie repeated her question to Ma.

'What do you mean, have I seen Rosalind? How would I have seen her?'

'She's disappeared.'

'*Disappeared?*'

'We think she might have been kidnapped.'

'Lord save us!'

Mabel dropped a plate, which broke into two pieces when it hit the ground.

'Never mind the plate, Mabel! Elfie, go fetch Pa. Quick now!'

Elfie rushed past as Joe brought the Trelawneys into the kitchen. It was the first time Clarissa had ever entered the *Pig and Whistle* but Elfie didn't have time to make her feel comfortable, Ma would do that.

Elfie raced up the stairs, taking two steps at a time and burst into Pa's study without knocking.

'Come at once, Pa! Rosalind's been kidnapped.'

He put down his pen and looked at Elfie over the top of his glasses. 'This is not your idea of a joke, Elfie, I trust?'

'Honest, cross my heart, hope to die, it's not!'

Pa followed Elfie down to the kitchen and greeted the Trelawneys briefly before asking to be told exactly what had happened. The expression on his face was grave by the time he had heard the whole story.

Clarissa's head was lolling back against her chair.

'Would you have any smelling salts, Mrs Bigsby?' asked Alfred Trelawney.

'Can't say as I have. Never had no need of them. A tot of brandy might do the trick. And a good cup of strong tea.'

Joe ran to fetch the brandy from the bar and Alfred Trelawney held the glass to his wife's pale lips. She coughed and her eyes fluttered.

'Rosalind,' she cried.

'It's all right, dear.' Her husband smoothed her brow. 'There will be a perfectly reasonable explanation for it all.'

Ma was at hand with the tea which she served in one of her rosebud china cups, the ones she brought out for special occasions. 'Try some of this, dear. It'll do you the world of good.'

No one disobeyed Ma. Clarissa took a sip, and then another.

'I think, Alfred,' said Pa, 'that we must telephone the school contacts without further delay. And if they are of no help then we must call in the police.'

'Liam went up the street not five minutes ago,' said Florrie, who had joined the company. 'He was on his way back to the station.'

Liam, Constable O'Dowd, known better on the beat as Dowdy, was Florrie's fiancé.

'Let us go at once and make the calls,' said Alfred Trelawney.

'Don't leave me, Alfred,' pleaded Clarissa.

'It's all right, dear,' said Ma, 'I'll look after you while your husband is gone.'

Clarissa still looked unsure but remained where she was and accepted another sip of brandy with her tea.

Her husband set off up the street, accompanied by Elfie, Joe and Pa Bigsby, who walked with straight back and measured step, his silver cane in his right hand. There was no good trying to make Pa hurry. He would just say that patience would get you there in the end.

Elfie felt exceedingly impatient. She reached the shop where there was a telephone box first and held open the door.

'I think perhaps it might be easier to let your father deal with this alone, Elfie,' said Pa.

She hopped about while her father was inside the shop. He kept his back to them so that they could not read the expression on his face.

'He's taking ages,' she complained.

'That is a good sign,' said Pa. 'It means he has been able to make a connection and has found someone at home.'

Eventually Alfred Trelawney turned around and made his way out of the shop. They saw immediately that he had not received good news.

'No help there! Neither Henrietta nor Mary saw Rosalind after school, though Mary thinks she saw her getting into a cab.'

The four of them stood in silence for a moment. Finally, Pa spoke.

'Now then, Joe,' he said, 'we won't waste any more time. Run to the police station and see if you can fetch Dowdy.'

Joe ran like the wind, with long, loping strides. Elfie went after him and although she was a good runner she was soon left behind. She decided to wait for them at the corner and catch her breath. She thought about Rosalind and wondered where she could be. Wherever she was, Elfie hoped she was not too scared. When Elfie had been Rosalind's age, she was living on the streets but Rosalind had always been protected from the harder side of life. Now she was plunged right into it.

Elfie heard footsteps and looked up to see Joe and Dowdy coming at a steady trot. Even Dowdy could not keep up with Joe's speed. Elfie followed them back to the *Pig*, where her father and Pa Bigsby were waiting.

Clarissa rose as everyone came into the kitchen.

'Well?' she demanded, looking directly at her husband, her face pale and her expression desperate.

'No luck, I'm afraid, dear.'

Clarissa fell back into the chair and Ma reached for the brandy glass once again.

'Now we must all stay calm,' she said. 'It won't help none if we don't.'

Dowdy had his notebook out, and was asking questions and noting down everything they knew about Rosalind's school and her movements that day.

'Hm,' he commented, frowning. 'Not much to go on, is there? No descriptions of the cabbie?'

'They all look alike,' said Elfie. 'Well, from what I've seen of them going past.' Dressed in black from head to toe, sitting on their boxes, up above the street. How would you know one over the other?'

'What do you think then, Pa?' asked Dowdy.

'At the moment, very little.'

Elfie, bursting with impatience, jumped in. 'She *must* have been kidnapped!'

'No "must",' reproved Pa. 'Let us not go that far.'

'What else could have happened?'

No one had an answer.

'Have you any relatives she might have gone to, Mr Trelawney?' asked Dowdy.

'There are only my wife's parents.'

'She would never go there,' declared Elfie. 'She hates them. She's told me!'

Pa gave her a stern look.

'It's true. They're a couple of horrors. Mr and Mrs Clarendon-Smythe! You know that yourself, Pa. He was so rude to you when he come here.'

'Came,' murmured Joe.

Elfie wrinkled her nose at him. It was hardly the time to be fussy about her grammar.

'So she weren't fond of them?' asked Dowdy.

'You can say that again!' Elfie rolled her eyes.

'Nevertheless, they should be checked out,' said Pa.

'That's very true,' agreed Dowdy. 'We must leave no stone unturned. Do they have a telephone?'

'Of course!' scoffed Elfie. 'They have everything.'

'That's enough, Elfie,' rejoined Pa.

Clarissa looked as if she would rather be anywhere but in this room.

'I think I should go and telephone them so that we can rule them out.' Dowdy tucked his notebook into his top pocket. 'We've got to check everything. Would you care to come with me, Mr Trelawney?'

Elfie's father looked uncomfortable. 'Preferably not.'

'They were against our marriage, you see, Constable.' Clarissa looked down at the floor, speaking in a small voice.

'They thought he wasn't good enough for her,' added Elfie indignantly, 'because his granny came from Bermuda.'

'I think we need go no further with that now,' interrupted Pa Bigsby briskly. 'I shall accompany you, Dowdy.'

Clarissa wrote the telephone number on a piece of a paper and the two men left. Ma Bigsby made a fresh pot of tea while they waited for their return.

They came back in half an hour.

'They were not in residence,' reported Pa Bigsby. 'They have gone to stay in the Scottish Highlands for a week, in a hotel called *Fishers*, in a place called Pitlochry. We spoke to a maid at the house. She said her name was Lizzie O'Shea.'

'She's a nice girl,' said Clarissa, nodding. 'She hadn't seen Rosalind then?'

Dowdy shook his head. 'No, ma'am. We called the hotel and spoke to Mr Clarendon-Smythe. He was of no help. Said he hadn't set eyes on his granddaughter for months. He and his wife are due back in London tomorrow.'

'So Rosalind must have been kidnapped,' insisted Elfie. 'I bet you tuppence she has!'

'But why would anyone want to kidnap her?' demanded her father.

'Ransom?' suggested Dowdy. 'That's usually the reason.'

Mr Trelawney pushed his hand through his hair. 'But I don't have any money! I lost nearly everything when I was cleaned out by that villain Basildon-Blunt.'

'The kidnapper might not have known that, though,' said Joe quietly.

Chapter Three:
The Ransom

The public bar of the *Pig and Whistle* was packed that evening. Soon there was standing room only and Ma had to bolt the door. Florrie's earrings birled madly as she moved up and down the bar. The news of Rosalind's disappearance had spread far and wide throughout the borough. A number of people even came in to report sightings of Rosalind.

Mr Huckleberry, the ironmonger, swore he had seen her in Church Lane around five o'clock, but under questioning from Dowdy and Sergeant Feather, who had come from the police station to join him, he had to admit that he was not totally sure.

'I did see a girl with long blonde hair tied back with a black velvet ribbon.'

'Rosalind has no such ribbon,' said her mother.

Mrs O'Grady, the confectioner, thought she had come in with a group of girls to buy striped rock.

'I doubt if that was Rosalind,' sighed her father.

Mrs Crabbit, a local gossip, who spent most of her day on street corners, had been speaking to someone who *thought* she'd seen a girl the spitting image of Rosalind going into the pharmacist's.

'I think you should accompany your wife home, Mr Trelawney,' suggested Dowdy once Mrs Crabbit had taken herself off. 'This can't be helping her. We'll carry on taking statements. And we'll let you know the minute we get any word.'

'We certainly will,' added Sergeant Feather. 'We'll get to the bottom of this, never fear! We've got a man checking out all the cabbies in north London.'

Elfie watched her father lead Clarissa out of the *Pig and Whistle*. They looked so weary. She wished she could do something to find her little sister, something to put the smile back on their faces.

After they'd gone, the two policemen made extensive notes about all the reported sightings and then Ma Bigsby came in and chased Elfie and Joe off to bed. The children were normally only allowed to come into the public bar on a Saturday evening for the weekly sing-song. Elfie was sure she would never sleep a wink but she was so exhausted that once she'd climbed under the bedclothes, she dropped off at once.

৩৫

Her father and his wife were back at the *Pig* by breakfast time.

'I hope this is not too early, Mrs Bigsby,' apologised Alfred Trelawney. 'But we've been awake half the night.'

'I ain't surprised. You'd be needing a bit of company. Come on, sit in at the table and share a bite with us. Move along now, children.'

Clarissa declared herself unable to eat a bite but her husband accepted a bowl of porridge.

'Ain't much room at the table,' muttered Ivy, shifting her chair reluctantly, which earned her a stern look from Pa Bigsby.

In the middle of the meal, Dowdy arrived. At the sight of him Clarissa half rose from the table.

'Have you news, Constable?'

'No yet, I'm afraid, ma'am.' Dowdy shook his head.

The light in her eyes died.

'But it's early days.' Elfie knew Dowdy was trying to be consoling. 'She's not been gone twenty-four hours yet.'

'It feels like a month!' Clarissa sank back onto her chair.

'I can understand how you're feeling, ma'am. We've got a couple of men checking out the shelters and doss houses this morning.'

'Doss houses! Rosalind would never set foot anywhere like that.'

'Mebbe not. But it don't do no harm to check. I myself will be going over to the school to question the girls in her class.'

Elfie thought he'd be wasting his time there, but she had enough sense not to say so out loud.

'I thought Joe and I would go to the office,' said Alfred Trelawney. 'We are on the telephone there.' He looked at Ma Bigsby. 'I was wondering perhaps if my wife . . .'

'I'll look after her, never you fear.'

'That is most kind.'

'I'm going with Papa and Joe.' Elfie jumped up. 'I've got to!'

For once Pa Bigsby made no objection and did not mention algebra or Latin. Even Ivy kept her mouth shut. After all, they were caught up in exceptional circumstances. The younger children were whispering in corners and listening in doorways and having to be shooed away by Ma. She didn't want them to start thinking that this sort of thing might happen to any of them. The thought made Elfie shiver.

She encountered Ivy when she was carrying the breakfast dishes through to the scullery.

Ivy said, 'You know, you might be next!' Her eyes gleamed with excitement.

'Whatcha mean?'

'Well, you're a daughter of Mr Trelawney too, ain't you?'

'He told you – he's not got any money!'

'Don't give us that! He rides about in cabs, don't he? Dresses like a toff. Her too!'

Elfie pushed past Ivy and dumped her pile of plates into the sink, running water noisily onto them. Ivy would love her to be kidnapped and taken out of her way.

'It's all right, Elfie,' said Ma, from the doorway. 'You can leave that. You look as if you're getting your front all soaked anyway. Your dad and Joe are wantin' to get away.'

Joe had already hailed a cab. As they were riding into town Elfie squinted through the window at all the cabbies sitting up high on their boxes. One of them, somewhere in the city, had snatched Rosalind from outside her school.

'Could be any one of them,' murmured Joe. He was watching too.

Alfred Trelawney sat opposite, lost in thought. His brow was furrowed and the skin beneath his eyes was hollowed and dark.

'We're here,' announced Joe finally, as the cab pulled into the kerb.

Alfred Trelawney's head jerked forward. He fumbled in his pocket and gave Joe some coins.

'Settle it, Joe,' he muttered and stepped out of the cab.

While the cabbie was looking for change in his leather bag Elfie took the opportunity to throw him a few questions.

'Do you ever go up Hampstead way?'

'I goes everywhere anybody pays me to go.'

'Ever come across a girl's school called Miss Thorpe's Academy for Young Ladies?'

The man thought for a moment. 'Rings a bell. Niver had a fare there, not as I can remembers.'

'You weren't up that way yesterday?'

'Can't say as I was. Hey, why you askin' all these questions?' He looked Elfie straight in the eye. 'Is it about that girl wot was kidnapped?'

'How did you know about her?'

'The coppers have been down at the ranks askin' questions.'

'Anyone give them any information?' asked Joe.

The cabbie shook his head and closed his money bag.

'Hey,' said Joe, opening the palm of his hand to show the coins lying on it, 'you still owe us a half crown.'

'Sure you can count?' sneered the cabbie, about to step back up to his box.

'Absolutely sure.' Joe put a restraining hand on the man's arm.

'Take your dirty hand off me!'

Elfie was about to leap to Joe's defence when Alfred Trelawney turned and said sharply, 'How dare you! Do what my colleague says! If not, I shall report you. I have already noted your number. I take it you do not want to risk losing your licence?'

'My dad's a lawyer.' Elfie couldn't resist putting her oar in.

The cabbie fumbled in the bag and tossed a half-crown piece onto the pavement. Then he leapt onto his box and cracked his whip.

'Scum!' he cried and spat as he and the cab lurched off into the stream of traffic.

'Scum yourself!' Elfie yelled back.

'We don't need to sink as low as he has, Elfie,' reproved her father.

When the cab was gone from sight Joe bent down and picked up the half-crown piece.

'I shall keep a note of his number,' he said quietly.

'You don't think he might be the one who took Rosalind away?' asked Elfie.

'No. But we won't ever want to ride in his cab again, will we?'

Joe spoke more and more like her father every day, thought Elfie. A mixture of her father and Pa Bigsby. He had dignity.

Joe led the way to the office taking the steps two at a time. Alfred Trelawney climbed the dark twisting stairs wearily, holding onto the bannister rail.

Elfie followed slowly. Looking down into the murky depths of the stairwell she spied Clarissa's forlorn straw hat but did not mention it to her father.

Joe unlocked the door of *Alfred Trelawney, Solicitor-at-law*, and bent down to pick up a long white envelope that lay on the mat.

'Post?' asked Mr Trelawney as he walked into the office with Elfie.

'No, delivered by hand. It's addressed to you, sir.' Joe handed it over to Mr Trelawney, along with an ebony paper cutter.

Elfie knew in her bones that this was going to be bad news.

So did Joe. She could see it in his face.

Her father slit open the envelope and withdrew a sheet of white paper.

'It's a ransom demand,' he said quietly, 'for ten thousand guineas.'

Chapter Four:
Ten Thousand Guineas

'*Ten thousand guineas*,' echoed Elfie. 'That's a fortune.'

'Can I have a look, sir?' asked Joe.

Alfred Trelawney held out the paper and Joe took it.

'What does it say exactly?' Elfie found she was trembling. She put her hand on the back of a chair to steady herself.

'Read it, Joe,' said her father.

'*If you wish to see your daughter alive again then be prepared to pay a ransom of 10,000 guineas. We will be in touch tomorrow to tell you where and when to leave the money. You will have three days in which to raise the amount.*

'*DO NOT CONTACT THE POLICE!*

'*IF YOU DO IT WILL BE ALL OVER FOR ROSALIND.*'

Elfie gasped and looked at her father. His face was ashen.

'What are we going to do, Papa?'

'I don't know!' He slumped down onto his chair. 'There is no way in the world that I could raise such a sum of money. I don't even have one hundred in the bank, do I, Joe?'

Joe shook his head. He was still studying the letter and had taken it over to the window where the light was better.

'It's been typed on a Standard Typewriter, I would say. And not all that evenly. A bit hit and miss in places.'

'So?' said Elfie impatiently. What was Joe on about?

'It would suggest the letter has been typed by someone who is not totally familiar with typewriters.'

'That could be half of London, couldn't it?' said Mr Trelawney. 'More than half.'

Nobody in the *Pig* used a typewriter. Pa always said it would never take the place of good handwriting.

'This person then – or persons,' continued Joe, 'cannot be aware that you lost so much money in Chancery Lane, Mr Trelawney. Or, at least, I presume that they didn't. Otherwise they would not have demanded so much.'

Elfie's father remained silent, staring into the middle distance, almost as if he was not listening. Elfie fell silent too at the thought of trying to get hold of so much money. They could have a whip around at the *Pig* but that wouldn't raise much. And her dad had already sold the joy of his life, his Renault car. She couldn't think of anything else that he could sell. But they would have to save Rosalind somehow!

'The letter is grammatically correct,' Joe observed.

Elfie rolled her eyes. Grammar? At a time like this?

'Not written by a cabbie presumably?' Mr Trelawney had found his voice. 'Or someone with little education?'

'I would imagine not.'

Joe turned the paper over and held it up to the light. 'No watermarks.'

Elfie was getting impatient with all this detail.

'Maybe if we let them know you don't have that much money, Papa?' she suggested. 'Then they might ask for less.'

'How could we let them know? We don't know who they are or where they are,' Joe answered.

'Joe is right,' said Mr Trelawney. 'We don't know them. They are invisible. That is what makes it worse.'

'They *must* have known Rosalind's movements.' Joe's brow was furrowed. 'They could have done a reconnaissance beforehand at the school and watched the children coming out.'

'Rosalind might just have been the unlucky one who got picked out,' put in Elfie, though she didn't really believe it.

'The cabbie had a note that was supposedly signed by Clarissa,' her father reminded her.

'It was obviously well planned,' commented Joe. 'The cab arrived just minutes before the real one and was waiting right in front of the gate, didn't you say?'

Alfred Trelawney nodded.

Elfie had had enough of this discussion. It was time to get a move on.

'So what *are* we going to do?'

Her father told her that there was nothing much they could do at present, not until the kidnappers got in touch again. They were completely at their mercy. He reminded her that the police were doing what they could, continuing to question pupils from Rosalind's school, and cabbies.

'And getting nowhere.'

'I know, Elfie.' Her father sounded weary.

'Should we let the police know about this?' Joe held up the ransom note.

'No!' Alfred Trelawney was vehement. 'We cannot take the risk. I think we have no option but to wait until tomorrow and see if they deliver a second note. That might give us a further clue.'

❧

Elfie couldn't sleep that night. She lay tossing and turning, thinking about the kidnappers coming at the dead of night to deliver their next deadly note. Ivy was snoring in the bed alongside her and every now and then Dora, one of the twins, would cry out in the middle of a dream. Elfie felt like crying out herself. Or screaming. The *Pig and Whistle* was dead quiet. The bar closed at ten sharp and by eleven Florrie had cleared up and gone home to her lodgings and Ma and Pa were in bed. Asleep. Everyone seemed to be asleep except Elfie herself.

Suddenly she lifted her head. She'd heard a movement

coming from the boys' room further along the corridor. She pulled a shawl round her shoulders and tiptoed out onto the landing.

Joe was coming towards her, fully dressed!

'What you doin'?'

'Shush!' He put a finger to his lips and beckoned her.

She followed him down the stairs. Some light was filtering in from the street lamps onto the landing.

They went into the kitchen.

'Where you goin'?' asked Elfie again.

'To the office.' Joe's intention was to wait and watch, in the hope of catching sight of the kidnappers as they delivered their note. 'I think they might wait until dead of night before they do it.'

'How you going to get there?'

'Some cabs run through the night. I've got money.' Pa Bigsby let Joe keep some of his wages. It was only fair, he said.

'I'm coming with you.'

'You can't, Elfie!'

'Who says?'

She dashed into the cloakroom, stuck her feet into her boots and pulled her coat on over her nightdress. Joe shook his head but said nothing more. He knew she wouldn't listen. She followed him out into the street.

It was raining slightly, gentle summer rain, kind on the face. The gas lamps glistened. The street seemed unreal, thought Elfie, compared to daytime when the pavements were busy and buses and carts careered along the road. Nothing was moving except for a ginger cat that slunk across the road to disappear into the shadows.

'Are you sure there'll be a cab?' Elfie peered along the street.

'There should be sooner or later.' Joe was standing on the kerb, turned to the right, watching. 'I've seen them when I've looked out of the window at night.'

A nearby clock chimed once.

'Quarter-past eleven,' said Joe.

A minute or two later they heard the rumble of wheels and the clip-clop of a horse's hooves.

A cab came into sight, its lantern swinging. Joe stepped out into the street and held out his hand. The cab didn't stop. Its curtains were closed.

'Scum!' cried Elfie.

Joe gave her a look.

A second or two later another cab came into view. Joe tried again.

This time the cab pulled in. The cabbie didn't slacken his reins, as if he might take off again at any moment.

'Could you take us to Holborn?' asked Joe. 'I've got the fare.' He opened his palm to show the cabbie the coins.

'*Please*,' added Elfie. 'It's an emergency. My auntie's sick as a dog and we're taking her some medicine. It's a matter of life and death.'

The man looked unconvinced but said, 'Give us the fare first then.'

While Joe paid him Elfie opened the passenger door

and got her foot on the step. She wasn't going to let the driver diddle them that way; take their money and then be off like a shot. She pulled herself up into the cab and held the door open for Joe. The cabbie deliberately cracked his whip before Joe could even close it. They hung on for a fast, choppy ride through the near deserted streets.

Elfie liked the streets at night. Everything seemed more mysterious. She'd been used to roaming them when she was living rough, in her old life, not that she would want to go back to that. Sleeping under bridges on freezing cold nights? That was no fun.

Nearer the city centre the traffic increased and there were a few more pedestrians about. They reached Holborn Viaduct in record time.

The street outside Alfred Trelawney's office was deserted, except for a drunk man lurching along on the opposite side. He didn't notice them. There was no sign of any movement around the main door of the building. They pushed it open and slipped quickly inside. It was never locked. There was no key. As quietly as they could, they groped their way up the stairs. The skylight offered little help.

Joe unlocked the door of the office and bent down straightaway to examine the doormat.

'Nothing there. They haven't been yet.'

'They might not come at all.'

'If they're serious they will.'

Joe lit the lamp in the little room at the back so that

no light would be seen from the front. They then took up their positions on either side of the window that looked onto the street.

Midnight chimed nearby. Elfie counted out each stroke. They waited and waited, and from time to time Elfie sighed. She wished she could be as patient as Joe.

'Half-past the hour.' Joe held up his watch to catch the little light that there was.

Two or three cabs passed down below, and a carriage with its two horses clip-clopping smartly along. Two men walked along the other side of the street and disappeared from sight.

'Stay still!' whispered Joe suddenly, putting a hand on Elfie's arm. He cocked his head. 'Can you hear anything?'

Treading softly, he moved towards the door. As he did so a shaft of white came sailing through the letter box to land on the mat. Joe leapt on the door and tugged it open, just in time to hear a clatter of heels on the stairs. He raced down after them but he was only halfway down when he heard the main door bang shut. By the time he reached it and looked out into the street there was no one there.

Elfie joined him, holding the white envelope in her hand.

Joe was angry that he had let the man escape. 'He must have come along the inside of the pavement where we couldn't see him from that window.'

'Should we open it?' asked Elfie, holding up the envelope.

Chapter Five:
The Demand

'Bring the money in five-pound notes to your office on the night of Saturday May 11. We will telephone you there after midnight and instruct what you must do.

'DO NOT CONTACT THE POLICE!

'IF YOU DO IT WILL BE ALL OVER FOR ROSALIND.'

Elfie shivered. *It will be all over for Rosalind.* The same menacing phrase as in the first ransom note. The night seemed suddenly to have turned colder.

'They wouldn't really kill her, would they, Joe?'

'They might.'

She knew what he said was true. She'd come across some hardened criminals when she'd hung out around the docks. Men who would stop at nothing to make a few pounds, let alone this kind of money.

'What's you two up to then?'

They wheeled around to face a police constable.

'Watcha doin' hangin' around at this time of night?'
He came a step closer. He eyed Joe. 'Hey, Darkie, do
you play in them minstrel shows then? Saw them once
in the music hall. Quite a laugh they were.'

Elfie froze. Her stepmother, Clarissa, had wanted to
hire a group of entertainers called the *Happy Darkies* for
Rosalind's birthday party last year, but her father had
objected. Clarissa had been annoyed, protesting that all
her friends hired them. They were in vogue. But Elfie's
father had been adamant.

'Joe ain't no minstrel,' Elfie told the constable. 'He's
going to be a lawyer.'

'And I'm going to be Prime Minister. I want to know
what your game is.' The constable shoved the baton into
Joe's chest and pushed him back against the wall.

'You can't do that,' cried Elfie, catching hold of the
bobby's arm. 'He ain't done nothing. And neither have I.'

'Tell that to my granny! She'd laugh fit to burst.'

Elfie thought he looked as if he himself might burst.
His body was thick and his fingers looked like greasy
sausages wrapped around the baton.

'I'm going to ask you again. Wot was you up to? Tryin'
to break in somewhere, was you? Looking for some poor
innocent so as you could rob him on his way home after
a night out?'

'We were in my father's office,' said Elfie indignantly.
She jerked her chin up. 'Up the stairs there. My father
is Alfred Trelawney, Solicitor-at-Law. You can go up
and check if you like.'

'Oh aye, at gone midnight. Wot do you think I am? An idiot.'

Joe had stayed very still, pinned against the wall, making no effort to release himself. He knew it was the best tactic. He could free himself if he needed to. Elfie was keeping a sharp eye open for cabs and when she spied one turning into the street she jumped swiftly into the gutter and stuck her hand out. The cabbie pulled in and eyed the group suspiciously.

'We've got money,' said Elfie. 'Show him, Joe. We want to go to Green Lanes. Stoke Newington.'

Joe opened his hand. A silver florin glinted in the light.

The police constable, distracted, let go of Joe, who sprang free and darted into the road.

'Will I take them?' the cabbie called down to constable.

'You might as well. They'd cost me nothing but trouble, I can see that.'

Elfie didn't hesitate. She had the cab door open in a flash, Joe joined her, and they were off, galloping back towards Stoke Newington and the *Pig and Whistle*.

As they were creeping in by the back door, they heard a noise coming from the kitchen.

'Somebody's up,' whispered Elfie.

Ma was in the kitchen in her white flannel nightgown. She turned and faced them, hands parked on her broad hips.

'And where do you think you two have been in the middle of the night?'

'Well, you see . . .' started Elfie, and then stopped.

Ma was looking fierce.

'You best tell me, Joe,' said Ma. 'Else I'll just get a right jumble of a story.'

Joe explained and Elfie kept her mouth shut, not an easy thing for her to do.

'Dear love us!' exclaimed Ma, as she subsided into her usual armchair beside the fireplace, lost for words. She kept shaking her head.

'I don't know what Papa's going to do,' said Elfie finally. She had kept quiet long enough. 'Where's he going to get all that money from? '

But Ma's concern was with Rosalind. 'That poor child! Only the Lord knows what she's goin' through. She must be terrified out of her wits.' She sighed and heaved herself back up onto her feet. 'We'd best get to our beds. Sitting here'll not get us anywhere.'

ฌ

When Alfred Trelawney arrived the following morning with his wife, Pa Bigsby asked Ma to give Clarissa a cup of tea and tempt her to eat something. She was looking pinched with the worry of it all. And no wonder! Pa took Elfie's father up to his study, along with Joe and Elfie, and once they were seated he broke the news about the latest letter. Trelawney's face crumpled and he put his head in his hands.

'What am I going to do? What can I do?'

'Oh, Papa!' Elfie knelt down and put her arms around him.

'We must say calm,' began Pa, 'and think how best to proceed.'

'We can't go to the police, Mr Bigsby. We simply cannot! They will kill her!' Mr Trelawney looked broken.

'Dowdy knows already,' Elfie reminded him.

'But not about the ransom note,' put in Joe.

'Alfred,' said Pa, 'do you know anyone who could help financially? Anyone at all?'

Mr Trelawney shook his head. 'No one!'

'It is a great deal of money.' Even Pa did not seem to have any ideas. He stroked his beard.

'I know someone who could help,' said Joe quietly.

'Who?' demanded Trelawney.

'Rosalind's grandfather.'

'That horror!' exclaimed Elfie.

Her father frowned at her.

'It is true that he is wealthy, though, is it not, Alfred?' asked Pa Bigsby.

'Yes, indeed he is. Extremely wealthy. But I cannot imagine asking him for anything. He hates me.'

Everyone knew why – Clarendon-Smythe hadn't wanted his daughter to marry someone he thought beneath her. All because his mother had come from Bermuda.

Elfie wanted to say something about people who judged you on your blood, but instead suggested that Clarissa could ask her father.

'He cut her off without a penny, remember. Closed the door in her face, told her he never wanted to see her again.'

'But surely,' said Pa, 'to save the life of his granddaughter, his own flesh and blood? He wouldn't be so heartless as to refuse, would he?'

'He's nasty enough,' Elfie reminded them. She loathed the man.

'He cannot be that evil,' objected Pa. 'He'd be a monster if he were. Besides, he has a certain standing in the community. If it were to be known that he refused to help secure the safety of his own flesh and blood, he would be totally disgraced.'

Elfie nodded. 'You've got a point there, Pa. Rosalind told me he hobnobs with a lot of bigwigs. She said he met Queen Victoria once. Before she died,' she added.

A small smile flickered over Joe's face.

'Perhaps, Alfred,' said Pa, 'you should discuss this with your wife?'

Mr Trelawney nodded. 'I must! He might be our only hope.' He rose from the chair.

Elfie's father left them to return shortly afterwards with a distressed-looking Clarissa. Pa rose, saying that they would leave them alone to talk. He would go and wait in the parlour with Elfie and Joe.

They waited in silence. The younger children were doing some colouring in, on picture books. Ivy and Billy were sprawled on the floor playing noughts and crosses. Lessons had been delayed. No one was asking why. No one was squabbling or making a noise. It was if all the orphans sensed that something serious was going on.

After what seemed like an hour, but might only have been a matter of a few minutes, Elfie's father put his head round the door. Elfie was up on her feet in a moment. Joe joined her and, along with Pa, they returned to his study. Clarissa's eyes were red and her cheeks damp with tears. Once they were all in the room, Joe closed the door and stood with his back to it.

Alfred Trelawney spoke first. 'Clarissa has agreed to ask her father.'

'What else could I do?' Her voice wavered as it rose. 'He must give me the money. He *must*. He couldn't let them kill her!' She broke down again.

Elfie knuckled her eyes. Pa blew his nose. Joe stared down at his feet.

'He must,' repeated Clarissa, dully this time.

But will he? wondered Elfie.

Clarendon-Smythe was a hard, proud man and she wouldn't be surprised if he had a heart of stone.

Chapter Six:
Clarissa Appeals
to her Father

Clarissa sat at Pa Bigsby's desk to write her letter. Her husband sat close beside her, his hand resting lightly on her arm. Pa put a brand-new nib into a pen and dipped it into the bottle of royal blue ink. Clarissa had shaken her head at the black ink which Pa himself used. It made her think of death, she said. Elfie shuddered.

'*Dear Father* . . .' Clarissa murmured the words aloud as she wrote. Then she stopped. 'He's not dear at all! I hate him.' She laid down the pen, sending a spattering of blue ink across Pa's clean blotter pad.

He did not look as if he minded about that.

Pa calmly picked up the pen, dipped it into the inkwell once more and placed it in Clarissa's hand.

'You can do it, dear,' urged her husband.

'Of course you can,' said Pa quietly.

'You must, my love,' added her husband. 'Think of Rosalind.'

They were all thinking of Rosalind.

'Tell me what I should say, Alfred.' Clarissa's hand steadied and she began to write again, very slowly and carefully.

Alfred Trelawney started to dictate but after '*Dear Father, I regret . . .*' he faltered too.

He took a deep breath and then continued in a stronger, firmer voice:

'*I regret to inform you that our very dear daughter Rosalind has been kidnapped. We have received a demand for ten thousand guineas in ransom, which we cannot raise. The kidnappers are threatening to kill her if we do not pay by the eleventh day of May. I know that you are very fond of your granddaughter and would not wish such a terrible fate to befall her. I beseech you, therefore, with all my heart and soul to come to our aid, to help us raise the ransom money.*'

Clarissa looked up. 'I don't know how to sign it. I cannot write *Your loving daughter*. I simply cannot! He knows I do not love him, Alfred. Not after I went against him to be with you.'

'If I may make a suggestion?' asked Pa.

'Please, Mr Bigsby.'

'I think it might be in order to say *Your respectful daughter*, even though I realise you do not truly respect him.'

'I certainly do not!'

'There are times when a little white lie is not only acceptable but essential.'

That was interesting, thought Elfie, as Pa was always such a great stickler for the truth. But she could see his point here.

Clarissa wrote the words he'd suggested and signed the letter. Pa blotted it carefully, making sure the ink was perfectly dry before folding the page in two and sliding it carefully into a long white envelope. He sealed it with red wax but did not put his personal stamp on it.

'Shall I write the address for you?'

'Please, Mr Bigsby, if you would.'

Alfred Trelawney dictated the address in Hampstead where Clarissa's parents lived and Pa wrote it in his fine flowing hand. No one could do such wonderful loops as Pa and his downward slopes were perfectly in line. Elfie knew she would never reach the same height of perfection even if she were to practise all day. She was bad with ink blots too, though not as bad as when she had first come to the *Pig*. She hadn't even known how to hold a pen then.

Pa handed the envelope to Joe and asked him to convey it forthwith to the post office.

'It should reach Hampstead by the afternoon post. I think your parents will have returned from Scotland by now, Clarissa?'

'Yes, that is what the butler said.'

Elfie went with Joe. They ran most of the way to the post office but walked back. There was no hurry now.

逃逃

The day crawled slowly by. Alfred Trelawney decided not to open his office but to go home with his wife to wait. Pa resumed classes but Elfie found it difficult to concentrate. Her eyes kept straying to the clock on the schoolroom wall. So did Joe's, she noticed. Pa had enlisted him to help the nine-year-old twins Nancy and Dora with their sums but he wasn't paying very much attention.

Pa was telling the older children about the Boer War, which might have sounded exciting except that a lot of men had got killed or lost limbs. Elfie had seen some of the survivors standing around street corners leaning on their crutches. One of the *Pig and Whistle*'s regulars, Dickie Dent, had even had a leg sawn off on one of the battlefields, with only a tot of brandy to help his pain.

'Let us hope that none of you young ones will ever have to go and fight in a war,' said Pa, 'and waste your lives for nothing. Best stick with the railways, Billy.'

Billy had talked about joining the army but he looked less sure after today's lesson.

It was time to move onto something more cheerful. Pa opened *Little Lord Fauntleroy* by Frances Hodgson Burnett. Elfie liked the story but even that was difficult to concentrate on today. Her mind was far away.

Where could Rosalind *be*? She tried to picture her little sister. Was she locked up in a dark room, blindfolded, crying out and nobody hearing her? Who were those dreadful people who would do such a thing? Nameless people without a face. Elfie sighed and her eyes smarted. She felt quite queasy with worry.

Ma put her head round the door.

'Dowdy is here, wantin' to know if there's any new developments.'

Elfie looked at Pa, whose face was expressionless. He didn't like interruptions at the best of times.

'I told him nothing much and you was teaching,' Ma went on.

'*Were*', Elfie mouthed. It had become a habit. Why didn't Pa ever correct Ma's grammar. Was it because she was Irish, like Dowdy? He didn't tick off Dowdy either.

'Tell him I'll call on him later,' said Pa finally and Ma left.

'I think –' he said, '– we shall terminate classes early this morning. Go quietly now, children! No need to run.'

When they had gone Pa came over to Elfie where she still sat at her desk and put his hands on her shoulders. By now, tears were running down her cheeks – she who so seldom cried.

'We shall find Rosalind, Elfie,' he said softly. 'I am sure her grandfather will give your father the money.'

Elfie lifted her head. Pa offered her the snow-white handkerchief he kept in the top packet of his lilac suit and had seldom been seen to use. She took it, wiped her eyes and blew her nose.

'Thank you, Pa.'

The door burst open. Ivy stood on the threshold.

'Ivy,' chided Pa, 'how many times do I have to tell you to enter a room in a more ladylike manner?' He often had to tell Elfie too.

'But, Pa, that old Ramsbum is here!'

'Oh, I see. But you should not refer to him in such a way.'

Pa was not angry though. He was stroking his beard and thinking. He was not at all pleased to have a visit from the schools inspector Mr Ramsbottom. Who would be? He was one of the most disgusting men Elfie had ever come across, and she had come across many in her life. The inspector had greasy hair and dirty fingernails and he smelt when he bent over your desk. There was a time when she might not even have noticed such things but Ma and Pa were both sticklers for cleanliness. Ma was forever demanding to see your nails.

Pa straightened his back. 'I shall have to send him away. We are in no state for an inspection today.'

'Shall I go and tell him?' asked Ivy.

'Certainly not. I shall tell him myself.'

The girls trooped down down the stairs after Pa. At the foot stood the inspector in his long greenish-black coat and filthy boots.

Pa got in the first word. 'Good morning to you, Mr Ramsbottom. I am afraid it is quite impossible for us to welcome you into the school today. We have an emergency on our hands. And, if you remember, I have asked you before to give us warning of your inspections in advance.'

'What use is that? Just gives you time to tidy up.'

'Are you suggesting, Mr Ramsbottom, that I keep an untidy and slovenly school?' Pa stared at the man with his piercing blue eyes. The inspector studied his dirty boots. 'That would be a slur upon my character which I could not tolerate. I should have to make a complaint to your superiors.'

The inspector took a step backwards. 'I was not suggesting anything of the sort. I was merely passing and thought I would look in.'

'Well, you've had your look now,' muttered Elfie.

The inspector's head jerked up. 'What was that, girl? I seem to recall that you can be impertinent.'

'I was just reciting a poem to myself. I love poetry, if you remember.' She had recited *The Daffodils* last time the inspector visited. Mr Ramsbottom had thought she wouldn't know any poetry so she had given him the lot, from start to finish.

'*I wandered lonely as a cloud*,' Elfie began.

'That's enough, girl.' Mr Ramsbottom sniffed. 'I'll come back another time, Mr Bigsby.'

'A good idea.' Pa edged the man towards the door. The inspector half tripped over the mat and almost fell. Pity, thought Elfie. She would have loved to have seen him sent sprawling. She and Ivy could scarcely restrain their giggles.

Pa closed the door behind the man.

'He's a right stinker, ain't he?' said Ivy.

'*Isn't*,' said Elfie. 'But yes, he is.'

'That is disrespectful of you, girls,' said Pa, but his eyes were twinkling. He had the kind of eyes that could twinkle. Not many people did, Elfie had observed.

Then Pa looked sombre again. For a few minutes their thoughts had been diverted from Rosalind's plight. Now it was the only thing in their minds again.

రారా

The reply reached the Trelawney's house just after eight o'clock in the evening. It was delivered by the Clarendon-Smythes' butler. The Trelawneys immediately summoned a cab and came to the *Pig and Whistle*.

Elfie saw straightaway that the reply did not contain good news. Her father and his wife looked as if they were ready to crack and fall apart.

'Won't they do it?' cried Elfie.

'Shush, Elfie,' said Pa. 'Let us go up to my study.' He called to Ma and Joe to come and join them.

They went upstairs. Joe closed the door and stood with his back to it. His eyes had that wide sombre look, as if he feared the worst. Elfie thought she might be sick.

Clarissa was helped into a chair, where she began to sob quietly, covering her face with a lace-edged handkerchief.

'I cannot believe they have turned you down, Alfred?' Pa frowned.

'Not exactly. May I read the letter to you?'

'Please do.'

'*Dear Clarissa,*

'*We were greatly distressed to learn of the kidnapping of our dear granddaughter Rosalind. I am of course prepared to pay the ransom of ten thousand guineas to secure her release.*'

'There you are!' cried Elfie. She punched the air.

'Wait!' Her father held up his hand, then continued reading.

'*I must lay down one condition, however, for the sake of Rosalind herself. The condition is this: that you sign over legal guardianship to her grandmother and myself.*'

There was a heavy silence before Elfie burst out, 'He can't make you do that!'

'There's more,' said Clarissa in a quiet voice.

'*Thereafter, Rosalind would live with us, and us only, and you would not be permitted access or should not attempt to see her. I do not consider either you or your husband to be suitable guardians for our granddaughter. We will rear her in a manner suitable for a member of our family and ensure that she moves in the right circles and is not subjected to the quite unsuitable company that your husband favours in low-down places such as public houses and the like.*

'*I will not waiver from this condition.*

'*I await your reply.*'

The letter was signed *Augustus Arthur George Clarendon-Smythe.*

'That's terrible!' Elfie could not quite believe it. Give Rosalind away? They couldn't do that.

'It is appalling.' Pa shook his head. 'That a man could deny a child her loving parents.'

'Can he get away with it?' asked Elfie. 'Stop Rosalind from seeing her mum and dad for ever and ever?'

'He can if he has a signed legal document. I am right, am I not, Alfred? You are the lawyer amongst us.'

'I'm afraid you are right, Mr Bigsby.'

'Don't sign it then.' But Elfie stopped. The alternative was even worse: to leave Rosalind in the hands of the kidnappers. They might even kill her.

Clarissa was shaking. Her husband steadied her and Ma came over to her chair to lay a hand on her shoulder. 'You poor lamb,' she said. 'Joe, away down and ask Florrie for a tot of brandy.'

Elfie went with Joe.

The bar was busy. It would not be long to closing time. Frankie was playing a tune on the harmonium and his friend Sad Sid was humming along to it. Florrie was working hard to fulfil the last orders while Dowdy leant on the bar, chatting to her whenever she came to rest in front of him.

'We're still not getting any breakthrough on your sister, Elfie,' said Dowdy. 'Dead sorry about that. The trail seems to have gone cold. It's a dreadful business so it is, that a young girl can just disappear like that into thin air. But we haven't had even a whisper, not since the first day when all sorts of people came in to say they'd seen a little girl just like her.'

Joe asked Florrie for the tot of brandy. 'It's for Mrs Trelawney.'

'Poor woman.' Florrie shook her head and her long pearl earrings swung and sparkled in the light. Elfie was going to get herself a pair like that when she was old enough. 'She must be going through hell,' added Florrie.

'We all are,' said Elfie.

On the way back up the stairs Joe, stopped briefly and in a whisper told her he felt guilty that he hadn't told Dowdy what they knew.

'You couldn't!'

'I know.'

They continued up to Pa's study.

Clarissa turned her head away at the smell of the brandy but Ma held the glass to her lips and there was no denying Ma anything if she had her mind set on it. A little colour returned to Clarissa's cheeks.

'What are we going to do, Alfred?' Clarissa's voice cracked.

'Your father won't change his mind, will he?'

'No, he won't. I know him too well. He definitely will not!'

'You could sign the form,' suggested Elfie, 'and then we could grab Rosalind back afterwards. When she's living with them she'll be desperate to come back home.'

'He would have all the might of the law on his side,' said her father. 'We could not win that one.'

'There really is no choice, I'm afraid.' Pa Bigsby's voice was grave. 'You must save the life of your child first and foremost. It might be possible afterwards to find a way to reclaim her.'

Alfred Trelawney did not look too hopeful. 'Clarissa's father is an influential man. He is powerful and wealthy.'

Elfie's mind was whirring. She was thinking, hoping, that snooty old Clarendon-Smythe might meet with an accident at some point. Or that Rosalind might run away and she and Joe would help hide her.

'You are right, Mr Bigsby,' said Alfred Trelawney heavily. 'We really do not have a choice. Not if we are to save my little girl's life.'

Chapter Seven:
Rosalind's Fate

There was another letter lying on the mat in the morning. Joe swooped on it. He and Elfie had accompanied Alfred Trelawney to the office. Pa Bigsby had given up objecting to Elfie missing lessons. He knew her mind would not be on mathematics or algebra, or even poetry, which she usually enjoyed. At present nothing in the *Pig and Whistle* was as usual. They were caught up in a terrible tragedy, for, whatever the outcome, as Pa had put it, it would not, *could* not, be a happy one. Even in the bar in the evenings voices were muted. It was known throughout the borough that no trace had been found of little Rosalind. People feared the worst for the pretty, lively little girl as if she were one of their own. Neither Joe nor Elfie had uttered a word about ransoms, though there were times Elfie had to bite her tongue to stop herself from spilling it all out.

'Open it, Joe, please,' said Elfie's father. His hands

were shaking too much for him to handle even the envelope.

Joe withdrew the single sheet of paper. 'Shall I read it, Mr Trelawney?'

'Please.'

'*Go to your office at midnight tonight. Bring the money with you in a black sack and wait until you receive a phone call. You will then be given instructions which you must obey to the letter. Otherwise, you will regret it.*

'*DO NOT CONTACT THE POLICE!*

'*IF YOU DO IT WILL BE ALL OVER FOR ROSALIND.*'

Joe peered closely at the paper. 'The letter "n" is getting fainter and fainter,' he observed. 'Must remember that. And the fact that it has been composed by someone literate.'

'What d'you mean?' asked Elfie. She admired Joe's powers of deduction.

'Look – the spelling's all correct, and the full stops are all in the right places.'

Elfie looked again, and nodded. Joe was right. There was a pause before her father spoke.

'Joe,' said Alfred Trelawney, 'might I ask you to copy out this letter so that we may send it to Mr Clarendon-Smythe?' He sounded as if he had a lump of lead stuck at the back of his throat.

'Of course.'

They didn't own a typewriter.

Joe sat at the desk and penned the letter. He had excellent handwriting, as smart as Pa Bigsby's own, Elfie noticed. She knew she would never reach such heights. Pa was always talking about reaching heights that you'd never dreamt of. It was a matter of perseverance and paying attention in class, according to him, and not skipping subjects like Latin and algebra – not that those would help with her letters, Elfie thought. She liked the history and English lessons best but Pa said you never knew what you might need in life.

At the foot of the letter, Joe wrote, *Received this a.m.*

'Will that do, Mr Trelawney?'

'That should be sufficient. Thank you, Joe. Send it by cab. It will be quicker than post.'

'Perhaps I should take it myself to make sure? One never knows about cabbies.'

'That's true. Yes, go with it.'

'Papa, can I go with Joe?' asked Elfie and then felt guilty. 'Or do you want me to stay with you?'

'No, no, I am fine here. I have other matters that I should attend to. And a client is coming at ten. A Mr Booth, who wishes to raise an action at the Court of Session. At least it's some business, and it will take my mind off . . .' He was going to have said 'Rosalind', of course, but could not get the word out. 'And take a cab back if there is no bus in sight.' He passed some money over to Joe.

Elfie kissed her father and gave him a fierce hug before leaving. Joe went ahead and by the time she reached the street he had flagged down a cab. Joe was good at getting cabs. He stepped straight out into the street and held up his hand. If the cab showed no sign of stopping he would jump swiftly aside to avoid being trampled by the horse's hooves. He was agile and had a way of dealing with trouble, whether it was nasty cabbies or knots of youths looking for a fight. There were a few of those around. Joe was tall, well built and strong, and more than one of their customers at the *Pig* had suggested to Pa that he should put him up for boxing. But Pa said he would never ever agree to any of his boys becoming a boxer, and ending up with addled brains.

Normally Elfie would have enjoyed a ride in a cab on such a fine spring day. The blossom was out, making the trees look frilly with their pink and white flowers. People had shed their heavy winter coats and were stepping out with a spring in their step. Elfie was not. She had a pit of dread in the bottom of her stomach.

The cab deposited them outside a large, grim-looking house with turrets and tall chimneys. Much of it could not be seen for it was shrouded by dark green trees and encircled by high iron railings. A gate, topped with nasty looking spikes, barred the way to casual callers. An iron chain hung at the side of the gate. Joe pulled it and a bell clanged. Elfie peered through the bars, watching the studded mahogany front door. It opened, and out came the butler in his black suit. He had a jowly face and cauliflower nose and Elfie thought he must be the man who had delivered the note to her father's house.

'That's Dimmock,' whispered Elfie. 'He's a horror, Rosalind told me.'

Dimmock made slow progress down the path. When he opened the gate and saw the visitors, his nose puckered into a sneer.

'Well?' He stared at Joe. Elfie was tired of people staring at Joe. Pa Bigsby said it was bad manners to stare at people. But she decided against saying anything on this occasion.

'We have a letter for Mr Clarendon-Smythe.' Joe held it out.

'Pass it through the gate if you please.'

'We're delivering it for Mr Trelawney. Rosalind's father, and mine,' Elfie said but Dimmock just waited until Joe did as he was told.

Were they not even going to get inside? Elfie could not believe it!

'Wait there in case my master should wish to send a reply.' The butler sounded sceptical about the likelihood of that. He retreated back up the path with the same slow gait.

'Huh!' Elfie parked her hands on her hips. 'You'd think he'd be a bit keener to save Rosalind's life!'

'Perhaps he does not know she is in danger? He is only the butler,' Joe said, but Elfie thought he must – how could he not?

She squinted through the bars of the gate again. Only the upper windows of the house could be seen and even then they were shrouded in some kind of gauze. At one window the curtain was partly drawn aside, held there by the hand of a girl. She had a pale face and frizzy red hair.

'That might be Frizzy Lizzie,' said Elfie. 'Rosalind told me about her. She's one of the maids. There are a couple of others, Mary and Dolly, who are nice, but the rest of the staff are all horrible.'

Elfie waved up at the window and, after a short pause, the girl lifted her hand in a limp greeting, then turned her back and disappeared.

'Lizzie would like to go home to Ireland but they won't let her,' explained Elfie. 'She was only twelve when they brung here here.'

'*Brought*,' said Joe automatically.

'Why doesn't she just walk out? That's what I would do.'

'She won't have any money,' said Joe, although he knew that would not have stopped Elfie.

'Here comes our friend.'

The front door had opened and out came Dimmock again, advancing slowly down the path towards them.

'Thinks he's somebody,' muttered Elfie.

Without a word the man pushed an envelope through the gate and returned to the house.

The envelope was addressed simply to 'Alfred Trelawney'. No 'Mr' No 'Esquire'.

'I suppose we'd better not open it,' said Elfie.

'Certainly not!'

They had to make their way back to Holborn now as fast as possible. Cabs did not loiter around a posh district like this touting for fares. These people would have servants for summoning cabs, if they didn't have carriages of their own.

'If we cut through to the High Street we can get an 83 bus,' said Elfie. She knew the area from visits to her father when he had lived nearby. In the days before his downfall.

As they reached the High Street they saw a yellow bus approaching.

'That's it!' cried Elfie.

They ran for it and leapt aboard, racing up the stairs to settle into the front seats. The 'garden seats', as they were known. For a few minutes Elfie forgot about Rosalind and her father and enjoyed the ride down Haverstock Hill through Camden Town.

They got off at the foot of Tottenham Court Road and ran the rest of the way back to the office, the letter gripped tight in Joe's hand.

Alfred Trelawney, who had been watching from the window, had the door open by the time they reached the top step. Joe handed over the envelope and Elfie's father slit it open at once with his paper knife.

I will come to your office at 10 a.m. tomorrow with my legal representative. He will have with him the document transferring the guardianship of my granddaughter Rosalind from you, Alfred Trelawney, to me.

'He's serious then,' said Joe.

'And he won't relent,' said Mr Trelawney. 'But it's the only way to save my daughter's life.'

~~~

Mr Clarendon-Smythe arrived as ten o'clock was striking in the local church. His lawyer, Mr Grimble, looked mean-faced. He examined the office with distaste. Elfie wondered how Clarendon-Smythe could collect so many ghastly people around him. Her father had allowed her to be present at the meeting, along with Joe. It was Saturday morning and a Mr Dawson was teaching Pa Bigsby's pupils to play cricket in Clissold Park. Pa valued cricket highly. Joe was an excellent overarm bowler and had once saved Elfie's life when a vicious criminal was holding a knife to her throat. Joe had bowled a lump of brick at the man and caught him right in the centre of the forehead. But today, neither she nor Joe had any interest in the sport.

Mr Clarendon-Smythe and Mr Grimble wasted no time. The lawyer withdrew a sheet of paper from his attaché case and laid it on Alfred Trelawney's desk.

'Sign there, please.' He stabbed the place with a hairy finger.

'I must read it first.'

Elfie and Joe stood on either side of Alfred Trelawney and read it also.

I, Alfred Trelawney, hereby fully and unconditionally agree to transfer the legal guardianship of my daughter Rosalind Margarita Trelawney to her grandfather Augustus Arthur George Clarendon-Smythe. I will not endeavour to obtain access at any time, nor to contact her in any way.

74

I waive all my paternal and legal rights as of now.

'I can't sign this!' Alfred Trelawney faced his father-in-law. He looked near to tears.

'In that case, Mr Grimble, we might as well go,' said Mr Clarendon-Smythe.

'You wouldn't let them kill her?' cried Elfie. 'Your own flesh and blood?'

Mr Clarendon Smythe looked at her as if she was dirt. 'She'd be better dead than in the care of a person like him.'

Elfie was taken aback by the venom in the old man's voice. 'He's my father.'

'Indeed he is. Illegitimately. That speaks for itself. What is it to be then, Trelawney?'

Chapter Eight:
The Decision

There was a long pause. The five people in the room were motionless. The cheap clock on the desk ticked the time away.

'I must –' Alfred Trelawney's voice cracked. 'I must save the life of my daughter.'

'In that case . . .' Mr Grimble laid the document back on the desk.

Trelawney collapsed into his chair and picked up a pen.

'Papa,' said Elfie, 'you can't let him have Rosalind!'

'I have to.'

'She'll be so unhappy. She'll cry her eyes out.' Elfie herself was spilling tears now.

Joe put his arm round her shoulder and steadied her.

'Let us waste no more time, Trelawney.' Mr Clarendon-Smythe was becoming impatient. 'Let us get this business over and done with.'

Trelawney dipped the pen into the inkwell.

'Sign there!' Grimble stabbed a broad finger on the line once again.

Rosalind's father inhaled as he braced himself, then he quickly scrawled his name. Elfie gasped. Grimble had snatched up the document in a trice. He blotted the signature and was now packing it away in his attaché case. He snapped the lid shut.

'We will see you here tonight,' said Mr Clarendon-Smythe, 'for the handover.'

Trelawney nodded and the men left. He, Joe and Elfie listened to their footsteps going down the stairs and then the main door banging shut.

'Strange,' mused Joe, 'that Clarendon-Smythe should have such a man as Grimble for his lawyer.'

Alfred Trelawney scarcely heard. He sat at the desk with his head propped between his hands while Elfie comforted him as best she could.

'We'll get her back, Papa. Don't you worry. Joe and I will find a way.'

✿✿

They assembled back in the office ten minutes before midnight, Alfred Trelawney, Elfie, Joe and Mr Clarendon-Smythe, the latter, this time, accompanied by his sour-faced butler as well as his lawyer. Their carriage was parked in a nearby side street and the coachman was at the ready to take off when instructed.

Mr Clarendon-Smythe threw a derisory glance at

Elfie and Joe when he arrived to find the children there, but made no comment. Joe had been worried that the kidnappers might have been watching the building and be apprehensive about having so many people around but Elfie wanted to be there for her father, and Joe for Elfie.

The small office was indeed crowded. Mr Clarendon-Smythe took Alfred Trelawney's chair without being invited, and without removing his top hat or gloves. The black bag with the money sat in the middle of the desk. Grimble sat in the seat reserved for clients while Dimmock stayed standing, feet apart, hands clasped behind his back.

Joe and Elfie leant against the back wall.

'It is imperative that no one makes a false move,' said Grimble.

Mr Clarendon-Smythe tapped on the desk with a gloved finger. Alfred Trelawney paced up and down the small space that remained. The minutes ticked slowly past. Elfie was so wound up she thought she might faint. Joe, as usual, stood still, seemingly composed, though Elfie noticed that his right eyelid twitched from time to time.

Midnight struck. Elfie counted the strokes inside her head. Twelve of them. Silence descended again, broken only by the sound of an occasional cab rattling past below. It was warm and stuffy in the small room. Elfie wished she could open the window and let in some air. It was a quarter past midnight now. Her father's face looked grey in the gaslight.

At twenty-five minutes past the hour the telephone shrilled, startling them all. Elfie's father lifted the receiver.

'Trelawney here.' His voice quavered.

He listened, his head bent, then said, 'I understand,' and hung up.

He turned to face the room.

'I have to take the money downstairs now and wait in the doorway. In five minutes a cab will come along and when it stops I have to cross the pavement and the cab door will be opened. I then put the money in and they will drive off.'

'But they might never come back!' cried Elfie. 'They could take off with all that money.'

'Hush.' Joe put a hand on her arm.

'What then, Trelawney?' Mr Clarendon-Smythe stood up.

'What about Rosalind?' Elfie could not keep quiet.

'They will take the money away and – if the amount is correct – the cab will return with Rosalind fifteen minutes later. We have no option but to trust them.'

'You'd better get down there now, Trelawney,' said Mr Clarendon-Smythe smoothly.

Grimble passed over the bag containing the money.

'We shall remain up here until the money is collected,' continued Mr Clarendon-Smythe, 'and then we shall come down the stairs. You, Trelawney, will come back up at that point and stay in here. Do not attempt to come back down. I repeat – do not attempt to come back down.'

'They're going to snatch Rosalind,' wailed Elfie, 'and take her away.'

'That was the deal,' said Grimble.

'The document is in my safe,' said Mr Clarendon-Smythe. 'If you endeavour to see or speak to Rosalind we shall not hesitate to bring a charge against you.'

Alfred Trelawney began to move towards the door. His shoulders were hunched.

'Let me come with you, Papa!'

'No, Elfie, I must do this alone.'

He left quickly. They listened to his feet as they went down step by step. Joe moved to take up a position at the window.

'Stay back from there!' barked Mr Clarendon-Smythe. 'You must not be seen. Go into the back room now, both of you!'

'Why should we?' demanded Elfie. 'This is my father's office.'

'Dimmock!'

The butler took Elfie by the shoulders and dragged her kicking into the back room.

'Tell him to leave go of her,' said Joe in a low voice. He took a step towards Mr Clarendon-Smythe.

'Are you threatening me?'

'Think you're strong, don't you?' Grimble rose to his feet and came towards Joe. He was half a head shorter than the boy. He took hold of Joe by the shoulders. Joe put out his hand and pushed him back. The lawyer hit his head against the wall and buckled at the knees.

'Stop this at once!' Mr Clarendon-Smythe smacked his cane across the desk. He would not tackle Joe himself. He might be large but looked as if he seldom took exercise.

Dimmock returned, patting his face with a handkerchief. 'She scratched me all over my face, sir. She's like a dervish.'

The marks were plain to see even in the flickering gaslight, and some were oozing blood, one close to his eye especially. But Elfie hadn't been silenced. She stood behind him, her hair on end, her coat torn.

'Enough!' declared Mr Clarendon-Smythe.

Elfie glared at him, daring him to send her out again.

Joe returned to the window.

'There's a cab stopping.' He shaded his face with one hand as he peered down. He could just make it out, a black cab and a single black horse. He saw a figure emerge from the pavement and move towards the cab. It was Alfred Trelawney. The cab door opened, Trelawney thrust the bag inside and the door closed.

'They've got the money,' reported Joe.

Alfred Trelawney was breathless by the time he reached the top of the stairs. He stood in the doorway, gasping. He held out his hands. 'I beseech you, Mr Clarendon-Smythe, please, please, for the love of God, let me claim my own daughter!'

But his pleas fell on deaf ears.

'She is my ward now.' Mr Clarendon Smythe brushed past him. 'You have been warned. If you attempt to interfere we shall have the law after you. Come, Mr Grimble. Dimmock!'

The three men descended the stairs. Joe and Elfie watched as their heads bobbed down the stairwell. Alfred Trelawney had subsided into his chair where he sat with his head bowed. He looked beaten.

Elfie gave Joe a look. 'I don't care, I'm going down,' she whispered.

'All right,' said Joe. 'But we mustn't mess this up.'

'I just want to see her.'

Elfie took off her boots and began to creep down the stairs in her stocking soles as fast as she could. Joe followed. They moved cautiously, and at the first landing, paused to look over the bannister. The three men were clotted together in a black lump in the main doorway. Joe and Elfie silently moved to the top of the last flight of stairs and crouched there, waiting. Two of the wall lights were out, the stairway was dim and creepy. Elfie slipped her hand into Joe's and he held it firm.

'Is that a cab?' Joe cocked his head.

There was definitely action below. Elfie and Joe peeped over the stairwell and saw Mr Clarendon-Smythe move out onto the pavement. The other two men hung back. Joe and Elfie tiptoed halfway down the last flight of stairs. They heard a cab door slam shut and then the other two men walked out into the street. Elfie and Joe reached the door in time to see Rosalind in the arms of her grandfather, her blonde ringlets falling over his shoulder. The cab that had delivered her was taking off and, a moment later, the Clarendon-Smythe carriage came rolling into view. Rosalind was sobbing.

'Rosalind!' screamed Elfie, rushing out into the street.

Rosalind looked round. 'Elfie!' she cried and struggled in her grandfather's arms, but he held her fast. She looked so small surrounded by the three large men.

'You'll only make it worse,' said Joe grimly, catching hold of Elfie's arm.

Mr Clarendon-Smythe passed Rosalind into the stout arms of the butler, who carried her into the carriage.

Elfie and Joe watched helplessly.

'Stay back,' warned Joe, keeping a tight grip on Elfie. 'We can't win. He'll have the law after your father. He could get him debarred – he could lose everything.'

The black curtain of the carriage was forcefully drawn across the window, obscuring the occupants within but not before Elfie saw her sister's hand slap at the glass helplessly. The coachman cracked his whip and the two black horses set off at a brisk pace.

Elfie turned and saw the haunted face of her father at the top window. The carriage and horses were gone now, and so was Rosalind. The street was empty.

Chapter Nine:
A Visit to
Hampstead Heath

Ma said you should always look on the bright side, that it didn't do any good letting yourself go too far down in the dumps, but even she admitted that it was difficult to see a glimmer of brightness in the present situation. Three days had passed since Rosalind had been carried off by her grandfather. The Ogre, Elfie called him now. 'The Horror' wasn't nearly strong enough.

'You can hardly believe a man would do such a thing to his own family,' said Florrie, for the tenth time. She had joined them in the kitchen for a cup of tea. After Rosalind had been returned, only to be taken away once more, the truth had come out about the ransom. There seemed little point hiding it now that Rosalind was no longer in danger. Dowdy had also arrived. He popped in several times a day to see if there were any further developments, as well as to see Florrie, of course. They were planning to get married in June and all the girls in the house, including Rosalind, were to be bridesmaids. Nobody was talking about that now.

'Some people are capable of the most dreadful things. Unfortunately.' Dowdy sighed. 'We see it all.'

'Can girls get to be coppers too, Dowdy?' asked Elfie.

He shook his head. 'They wouldn't be strong enough.'

Elfie snorted.

There was a knock on the door and Florrie jumped up to admit the Trelawneys. Elfie flew to her father and hugged him. Then she turned and after a moment's hesitation hugged her stepmother, for the first time ever. Clarissa had obviously been crying.

'Clarissa has been to see a friend whose daughter attends the same school as Rosalind,' said Mr Trelawney. 'She'd hoped to get some news of Rosalind.'

'And did she?' asked Elfie.

'She told me that Rosalind was no longer a pupil there.' Clarissa was close to tears again. 'She's been withdrawn. It's as if she's vanished. I may never see her again! Why is my father treating me like this?'

'Come on, luv,' said Ma, putting an arm round Clarissa's thin shoulders. 'Sit yourself down and I'll pour you a wee drop of tea with a tot of brandy in it.'

'I'll fetch the brandy.' Florrie went straightaway. It was becoming a regular trip these days.

Ma helped Clarissa into a seat and Elfie got a rose-patterned cup from the corner cupboard.

'What school has she gone to then?' asked Pa Bigsby.

'None,' Mr Trelawney replied. 'Apparently Mr Clarendon-Smythe told the headmistress she was to be tutored at home from now on.'

It was getting worse and worse, thought Elfie. Not only was Rosalind shut up in that big stone pile of a house but she wasn't being allowed to go out to see her friends. She must be terribly lonely, apart from missing her mama and papa.

Florrie brought the brandy and then returned to the bar. It was Saturday, which was always a busy night with lots of sing-songs and the occasional recitation from Mad Meg. She particularly loved *Roses are red, violets are blue*.

'Off you pair go and get some fresh air,' said Pa Bigsby. 'You've been mixed up in things you shouldn't even know about. It's time you had a break.

Elfie's father nodded. 'I don't know what I'd have done without you. But it's a lovely spring evening. Mr Bigsby's right.'

Elfie and Joe left and went for a walk up to the park.

'We've got to do something,' said Elfie, for what seemed like the millionth time. 'We could go over to the house. We might be lucky and catch sight of her at a window.'

Joe didn't need to ask who Elfie was talking about.

Rosalind might be looking out, hoping to see a familiar face. What would her grandparents have told her? That her parents had died? The Ogre was capable of anything, in Elfie's opinion. Joe's too.

'Let's give it a try,' he agreed. 'We could go tomorrow afternoon.'

Elfie normally spent Sundays at her father's house but he was taking his wife to spend a few days with friends in Brighton. He thought it would be good for her to get out of the house and the city and walk beside the sea and breathe the fresh salt air. Clarissa hated being alone in their house so she came every day now to sit in the *Pig's* kitchen. Ma Bigsby did not mind. She opened her arms to everyone in need, with one or two exceptions. Some of the pub's clients who were poor souls were always wanting to relate their woes but once they were let in to sit by the fire they wouldn't budge for the rest of the day. They smelt too: that was another problem. Ma said she had to draw the line somewhere.

After lunch the next day, which on Sundays was a special meal with roast beef, roast potatoes and Yorkshire pudding, Elfie and Joe set out.

Hampstead Heath was busy. Children played on the grass. Some flew kites while their parents lolled nearby enjoying the sunshine. Elfie and Joe scanned the heath carefully, though they knew there would be little chance of seeing Rosalind there.

There was no sign of any movement at the Clarendon-Smythe house. You'd hardly think anybody lived there at all. After taking a quick look through the bars of the gate Joe and Elfie kept back behind the wall, not wanting to attract the attention of Dimmock.

'There must be a back entrance,' said Joe. 'Why don't we go and take a look?'

The high wall shielded them all the way round. When they found the back entrance it, too, was hidden behind a high locked gate, and this one did not have bars to look through. It was made of stout solid oak.

'I suppose we couldn't climb over?' suggested Elfie.

'No, we couldn't!'

Suddenly they heard footsteps coming towards the gate. Joe seized Elfie by the hand and dragged her back round the corner.

'Wait,' he whispered. He risked a peep. 'It's that girl, the one we saw at the window.'

'Frizzy Lizzie?'

Joe was right. The girl closed the gate behind her and started to walk in their direction. They stood their ground. She stopped dead when she met them head on at the corner. Her eyes went at once to Joe's face. She put her hand to her mouth.

'It's all right, Lizzie,' said Elfie. 'We won't harm you.'

'How do you know me name?' The girl was wary and looked as if she could cut and run at any moment.

'Rosalind told me about you.'

'*Rosalind*?' Lizzie's eyes widened.

'She's my sister. My half-sister.'

'Are you Elfie? She's talked about you.'

'We'd like to talk to you.'

Lizzie glanced behind her. 'We can't stand here. I'd be

in big trouble if they were to see me talking to anybody, let alone you.'

'Can we go somewhere?' asked Joe.

'Come with me.' Lizzie was not wearing her uniform. She was dressed in a brown and white spotted dress and a thin brown cotton jacket. Her eyes were brown too and she had a spatter of freckles on her nose and across her wide cheekbones. She walked quickly down a back lane, until she was sure they were out of sight of the house. 'I've the rest of the day off. It's me half day and I were meant to be done long afore this but one of the maids, Dolly, took sick, so I had to stay and help out.'

'How is Rosalind?' asked Elfie urgently.

'Oh, she's in a terrible state, the poor child. Crying her eyes out half the day. It was a dreadful thing to happen to her, was it not? Her parents getting injured like that.'

'Injured?' queried Joe.

'In the accident. When their carriage overturned. Says they was hurt really bad and no one knows if they'll ever leave the hospital.'

'Liars!' Elfie was outraged. But Joe gave her a look. He was always so much more measured than she was.

'Let's tell you what really happened, Lizzie,' said Joe.

Lizzie listened in horror as Joe explained exactly why Rosalind was now living there. 'What a dreadful thing to do! It's criminal, so it is. They should be put behind bars.'

'I wish they were,' said Elfie fervently.

'Don't tell Rosalind everything we've told you,'

cautioned Joe. 'If you do she might blurt it out and then Clarendon-Smythe and Dimmock will be after us.'

'Dimmock! He's a dreadful man, so he is. You don't want to get on the wrong side of him, let me tell you.'

'We already have,' said Elfie.

'I 'ates him! He's nasty, like Quirk, the manservant. Slimey kind of a fellow.'

'Does Rosalind get to go out ever?' asked Elfie.

'No, never. She's like a prisoner in that 'orrible house. The housekeeper Mrs Dimmock keeps an eye on her. T'isn't right keeping the child locked up in the attic like that.'

Elfie couldn't stand the thought of Rosalind being shut up away from everyone else.

'Does Rosalind talk to *you*, Lizzie?' she asked.

'When her grandparents aren't around, or that old dragon what looks after her and gives her lessons.'

This was sounding worse and worse.

'What has she told you?'

'Not much, poor love. She wants to go and live at the *Pig*, whatever that is. When she says the name she bursts into tears.'

Joe and Elfie told Lizzie about the *Pig and Whistle* and Ma and Pa Bigsby.

'Sounds real nice, so it do,' said Lizzie wistfully.

'Why do you stay here, Lizzie?' asked Elfie. 'If it were me I'd be off.'

'I've no choice, 'ave I? I can't go home to Sligo. My father would kill me. I have eight brothers and sisters and I send money home every month. An agency in the city got me this job – ain't no good complaining.'

Elfie had come across Irish girls like Lizzie before. They'd run away from jobs after they'd been knocked about by their employers but when they'd complained to the agency they'd been sent on their way with nothing. They had ended up sleeping rough and begging.

'Perhaps . . . you *could* tell Rosalind you met us.' Joe changed his mind. 'If you get a quiet moment with her.'

'It might cheer her up a bit,' added Elfie, 'just to know that we're thinking of her.'

'But tell her to keep it to herself,' Joe cautioned.

'What should I say about her parents? She thinks they might die.'

Joe thought for a moment. 'You could say that we told you they are getting better but they can't have any visitors. Tell her not to ask her grandparents about it and you'll get the news from us.'

Elfie thought that would work. Joe seemed to have thought of everything.

'You could ask her questions about the kidnapping to try and distract her. Where she was taken, and by whom. Any details at all.'

Elfie couldn't see the point of that, but Lizzie nodded. 'I'll do that. All she's said is how she was rushed away in a dark carriage. There was a woman there wearing a hat with a veil but she never saw her face.'

'Could we meet you here again, Lizzie?' asked Joe.

'Next Sunday, if you like. Three?' She seemed pleased at the prospect of their company.

'That'd be great,' said Elfie.

They parted. They wondered where Lizzie was going to spend her free afternoon. Perhaps she was just glad to get out of that gloomy house for a while and walk in the fresh air.

Elfie and Joe couldn't get away from the Clarendon-Smythe house quickly enough.

'Poor Lizzie,' sighed Elfie.

'Poor Rosalind,' said Joe.

'It's dreadful, isn't it?' Elfie could imagine it now; Rosalind trapped up there like a princess in a tower. Did she even have her dolls to play with?

'At least we have a contact inside the house now,' said Joe as they headed back towards Hampstead Heath. 'That's a start.'

Of what? wondered Elfie.

Chapter Ten:
Lizzie Gives Them a Lead

The following Sunday they were in the alleyway a quarter of an hour early. Three o'clock passed without any sign of Lizzie. Elfie was getting anxious and beginning to hop from one foot to the other. Standing still did not come easily to her, as it did to Joe. He consulted the fob watch Pa Bigsby had given him when he started work.

'Plenty of time yet.' Joe's patience made Elfie even more impatient.

Lizzie arrived at twenty-past three, running and out of breath. 'I'm dead sorry, so I am.'

'That's all right, Lizzie.' Elfie took her hand.

'That woman always finds something to keep me back.'

'Mrs Dimmock?'

Lizzie nodded.

'Did you have a chance to talk to Rosalind?' asked Joe.

Lizzie had. After glancing to her right she moved closer to them so that they stood in a huddle. She then began to tell them what Rosalind had told her.

'She were scared out of her wits, of course – who wouldn't? – when she was snatched outside her school and bundled into a cab.'

'How many kidnappers were there?' asked Joe.

'Two, a man and a woman. The man had a scarf over his face and the woman was wearing a black veil.'

'What did she say about the journey?'

There was a pause while Lizzie recalled her conversation. 'It seemed quite long to her. The curtains in the cab were drawn so she couldn't see out. She screamed at first and the woman threatened to gag her. They held her down on the seat between them.'

'If we ever get our hands on those two thugs!' Elfie made a fist of her hand,

Joe carried on with his questioning. 'Did the kidnappers speak to Rosalind at all, or to each other?'

Lizzie related the rest of Rosalind's story, what she knew of it.

The man had not said a word to Rosalind and the woman only spoke curtly, to tell her to be quiet and sit still. After they had been travelling for quite a long way Rosalind became uncomfortable. She waited and waited and then she blurted out that she needed to go to the lavatory. The woman told her she couldn't. There were no WCs along the road. Rosalind waited a little while longer and then cried out that she *had* to go, she was going to burst. The man swore. Rosalind started to cry. The woman then said irritably, 'Oh, all right.'

The man thumped on the ceiling of the cab with his cane and then stuck his head out of the window to call up to the cabby. The horses came to an abrupt halt, throwing them forward. For a moment the woman's veil flew up and Rosalind saw the woman's face fleetingly. Her impression was that the chin was sharp and the mouth thin-lipped.

The woman ordered her not to dare try to run away. But Rosalind had no thoughts of doing that. She knew she would never outrun them. And she was exhausted and terrified.

The woman climbed out first, and the man helped Rosalind down. It was still daylight. The woman seized Rosalind's hand and drew her into a group of trees close to the roadside. They had left the city behind.

When Rosalind was ready, her kidnapper took her by the hand again and led her back to the cab. Rosalind just had time to glance around as they emerged from the wood and saw, to her left, a milestone at the roadside. It said: 'Barnet, 2 miles'.

Once back in the cab, they set off again and after a little while turned off the main road. Rosalind was aware of the change. The road beneath them became rougher. The wheels rumbled and their pace slowed.

And then the carriage came to a stop.

The woman said, 'You are going to stay in a house here for a few days. Until your pa pays the money.'

Rosalind told them that her papa did not have any money but the woman said he'd have to find it somehow or else it would be the worse for her.

The man opened the cab door and jumped down. He held out his hands to take Rosalind's. She saw that they were in front of a small red-bricked cottage and the nameplate on the door said Willow Tree Cottage. Before she had time to notice anything else she was pushed inside. The woman followed and the door closed behind them. There seemed to be no one else in the house.

The woman prodded Rosalind in the back. 'Go up the stairs, girl.'

The staircase was steep and narrow. Rosalind stumbled up. They went into a low attic room, lit only by a skylight. This was where Rosalind was to stay for the next four days, during which time she saw only the veiled woman, who brought her meals and took her downstairs to the bathroom. She was told that if she behaved herself there would be no trouble.

Elfie and Joe listened to the story in silence, horrified by what Rosalind had been through. But they were full of admiration too. She was only nine years old and had always been sheltered from the rougher side of life. She had never been left on her own and she was familiar only with the better-off parts of the city, apart from Green Lanes when she came to the *Pig*, and even then she didn't go outside alone. But it sounded like she had tried to pay attention to what was happening to her in spite of how scared she must have been.

Joe was first to find his voice. 'She told you a lot, didn't she, Lizzie? She must trust you.'

Lizzie looked pleased at Joe's compliment. 'I think she does. I egged her on, kept asking her to try and remember.'

'Did she tell you anything else?' asked Elfie.

Lizzie thought for a moment, and then said, 'Oh yes, she climbed onto a chest of drawers one day and were able to reach the skylight. She was all pleased with herself, said she must've grown. She got the window open and pulled herself up so as she could see out. It were in the middle of the country, the house, with no others round about.' Lizzie paused, then went on. 'And there were a barn alongside, and a wood.'

'I think you've put ideas into Rosalind's head, Elfie.' Joe smiled. A year ago Rosalind would never have dared to do such a thing. She had grown up a lot.

'If it was me, I'd have climbed out the window,' returned Elfie but she felt proud nonetheless.

'I think when she was in all that fresh air and green countryside she realised there was no chance of being rescued, or of escaping neither.'

'Keep talking to her when you can,' urged Joe. 'Asking her what she can remember.'

'I will.'

'Did you tell her you spoke with us?' asked Elfie.

Lizzie nodded. 'She was really pleased about that. She brightened no end, especially when I told her the bit about her parents. Said to ask you to rescue her.'

'That's not going to be easy, I'm afraid,' said Joe. 'Clarendon-Smythe has the law on his side.'

But Elfie wasn't going to allow her spirits to be dampened and she hugged Lizzie, thanking her for everything she was doing for Rosalind.

'I'd best be going now,' said Lizzie. 'I'm meeting my friend Kathleen. She has Sunday afternoons off as well.'

'Will you meet us here next Sunday?' asked Elfie.

Lizzie nodded. 'Same time.'

'And tell Rosalind you saw us again. Give her a big hug from us.'

'I'll do that.'

Lizzie left them. Joe and Elfie decided to walk part of the way home.

They struck down through the heath and then turned eastward, zigzagging their way through the streets of Tufnell Park. It was a good afternoon for a walk and families were out, some sitting in their doorways, enjoying the May sunshine. Joe had a good sense of direction and he said, if they kept going due east, they should more or less hit Green Lanes.

While they walked, they mulled over what Lizzie had told them.

'I think we should go and see if we can find Willow Tree Cottage,' said Elfie.

'I'm not sure what good that would do now.'

'Aren't you curious?'

'Yes, of course I am.'

'Well then!'

'It'd be like looking for a needle in a haystack. Willow Tree Cottage. There could be dozens around.'

'It's near Barnet.' Elfie was determined.

'That's a start,' admitted Joe. 'But if we did by some fluke manage to track it down we couldn't just go barging up to the door. No, you couldn't, Elfie!'

'I'd love to get my hands on that woman!'

'I know that.'

'If we could find the kidnappers we could get the money back, give it to the Ogre and get Rosalind back home again.'

'Yes . . .' Joe was looking preoccupied.

'We could go on Saturday. We can get a train from King's Cross. Are you on, Joe?'

'I'll have to think about it.'

'You're always thinking! No wonder Papa says you're going to make a great lawyer.'

ഹഈ

They had started supper by the time Elfie and Joe reached the *Pig and Whistle*. On Sundays, after such a big lunch at midday, they had only a light supper of bread and cheese and pickles. The meat had been good that day. Ma had her own special way of finding cheap cuts and making them tender. She would wallop them with a heavy wooden mallet.

'And where in the name have you two ragamuffins been?' she demanded, as they came into the kitchen. 'Do you see the time?'

'Just walking.' Elfie avoided Ma's eye.

'We was beginning to think you'd been kidnapped and all,' giggled Ivy.

Pa reprimanded her with a stern look, letting her know that he did not find her remark funny.

'Did you go walking anywhere in particular?' he asked, turning his attention to Joe and Elfie.

'Not really.' Elfie shrugged. 'All over, sort of.'

Pa regarded her with one raised eyebrow. He had a sixth sense which enabled him to suspect when they were up to something. Elfie knew that he would never give them his blessing to embark on an outing to Barnet to try to track down Rosalind's kidnappers. Luckily he let the matter drop, for the moment at least.

Neither Joe nor Elfie did. While they ate their bread and cheese, they thought of Willow Tree Cottage set at the edge of a wood, with a barn alongside, a little more than two miles from a place called Barnet.

Chapter Eleven:
Willow Tree Cottage

Clarissa had stayed on in Brighton with their friends for another week while her husband returned to town. He planned to rejoin her on Saturday, which was helpful for Joe, as it meant that the office would be closed again. As Alfred Trelawney said, they were not exactly swamped with clients so it would not make much difference to the business.

King's Cross station was busy when Elfie and Joe arrived. A lot of other people were heading for outings into the countryside. Whole families queued at the ticket office. Some carried picnic baskets over their arms. Elfie was excited. She loved the idea of travelling and fancied the idea of a picnic basket herself. She loved the shrill sound of the guards' whistles, signalling that another journey was about to start. The fire would be stoked until it glowed bright red and the big engine would heave into life and begin to chug forward, with sparks flying and plumes of smoke gushing from its funnel.

Elfie had never been further than the outer suburbs of the city of London, and then they had gone by bus. Pa Bigsby took them on outings whenever he could but there were so many in the family that it cost a lot in fares. One day, though, he was going to take them to the Lake District way up in the north, to see Wordsworth's daffodils – just like in the poem. He had promised that he would. He was putting a little money aside each month into a special bank account.

Joe had money in his pocket today and could pay for two return tickets to Barnet, with some left over. Two of Mr Trelawney's clients, who had been owing substantial amounts for some time, had finally paid.

The queue at the barrier was lengthy but once they were through Elfie managed to duck in and out of the crowd and scurry ahead to grab two window seats. She sat throughout the journey with her nose pressed against the windowpane. She didn't want to miss anything, not even the sheds and old warehouses that lined the first part of the track. Gradually though, as they moved further and further out of the city the scene became more interesting. There were houses with back gardens and flowers blooming brightly. Little children stopped playing to wave at the train. Elfie waved back.

It was nine miles to Barnet. Elfie wished it could have been ninety. After what seemed like no time at all, with a few stops at stations in between, they arrived.

Joe already had a plan of campaign, as Elfie had expected. They would go first to the post office – every place had a post office – and after the usual suspicious glances they always got, they would make their enquiries.

They found the post office easily enough. The man at the counter looked them over, Joe especially, of course, and asked what he could do for them.

'We're not wanting to buy stamps,' said Elfie and stopped. She did tend to say too much and give too much away.

'We're looking for a house called Willow Tree Cottage,' said Joe in his politest voice. And he could be very polite. His voice was deep and strong. Elfie's tended to rattle at times. Pa Bigsby was always telling her to slow down.

'Do you know it?' asked Elfie.

'Believe there are a couple of places in the area. Outside of the town. What are you wantin' to know for?'

'A friend of ours said her cousin lived there,' said Elfie, avoiding Joe's eye. 'She asked us to look them up and pass on a message.'

'Do you know what they're called?'

''Fraid not. She just said Willow Tree Cottage.'

'I see.' The man pursed his lips. 'So you know nothing about them? Not even their name?'

'Not really. But it is quite urgent, though.' The man did not look too convinced so Elfie added, 'And confidential.'

'Hang on a minute. I'll ask Bob through the back.'

He disappeared through a swing door.

'You are dreadful, Elfie,' whispered Joe.

'We'd never get anywhere though, would we, if I didn't –'

'Lie,' finished Joe.

'It's in a good cause.'

'I know. At least I hope so. He might be phoning the police station while he's through the back to say he's got two suspicious characters out here.'

'That's your fault then. You could paint yourself white.' Elfie dodged out of reach of Joe's arm.

The man returned a couple of minutes later with Bob, who was wearing a postman's uniform.

'You're looking for Willow Tree Cottage?'

They nodded.

'I deliver to a couple of houses with that name. Not too often. Just now and then. One's about a mile out. The other's two, maybe three, in the opposite direction.'

'Could you tell us how to find them?' asked Joe.

'Hang on, I'll draw you a map.' He found a piece of paper and a pencil. 'Turn right as you leave the houses, then carry straight on. I'll show you where the other one is too. Best try the nearest one first. More sign of life there.'

They thanked him for his trouble and set out, armed with his maps. It was a nice day for a walk in the country, with all the spring flowers out. They could recognise daisies, dandelions and buttercups, but none of the others. Not many flowers flourished in Stoke Newington though Ma did grow geraniums in barrels outside the *Pig and Whistle*.

Elfie picked a buttercup and held it under Joe's chin to see if it would shine.

'You like butter!' she told him. Florrie had taught her that. Florrie had lived in the country for a while as a child before her parents moved into the city to look for work.

The first cottage was easy to find. They met a man on the road who confirmed that they were going in the right direction.

'Turn left at the next lane and you'll be there.'

As they drew near they heard children's voices. They looked at each other. This didn't sound too promising. Rosalind would surely have mentioned other children to Lizzie. When they reached the end of the lane they saw half a dozen children playing on the grass, while another swung on a rope from the branches of a stout apple tree. There was no barn, no wood, and no sign of a willow tree, although the nameplate did say Willow Tree Cottage.

'This ain't it,' said Elfie.

'*Isn't*,' said Joe.

A woman was standing in the doorway holding a baby in her arms. She stared hard at Joe but then everyone did. Perhaps they didn't see many black people in the country. Perhaps they didn't see many strangers at all. The children had stopped playing to gape at them too.

Elfie did the talking. 'We're looking for a house called Willow Tree Cottage.'

'Oh yes?'

'A friend in London asked us to call on her cousin.'

'I ain't got no cousin. You've come to wrong place. So you're from London, are you?'

The way she said it, it was if she thought they'd come from the moon.

'I think we must have got the wrong house. There's another one a couple of miles away, so we were told?'

'I wouldn't know about that. What do you call them?'

'It's all right,' said Elfie, backing off.

'Sorry to have troubled you,' said Joe.

'That's all right,' said the woman, but she stayed where was, watching them go.

It took them well over an hour to find the second cottage. The postman's map was not very clear and they had to stop at a couple of houses along the way and ask for help. Elfie did the asking while Joe stayed out of sight.

At last they stood in front of a house that matched Rosalind's description. It was red-bricked, bore the name Willow Tree Cottage above the door, had a wood at the side and a barn. And in the middle of the garden stood a solitary drooping willow tree.

'This must be it!' declared Elfie triumphantly.

There was no sign of life here, no children playing, and the front door was shut. Net curtains draped the windows.

They had agreed that this time Elfie would go alone to

the door while Joe stayed back at the edge of the wood, but well within earshot in case she needed help.

Joe concealed himself in a clump of trees and Elfie made her way up the path to the front door. She lifted the brass knocker and tapped three times. Nothing happened. She knocked again, using more force this time, and a moment or two later the door opened.

A tiny, white-haired, spectacled lady, peered out at her, leaning on a stick. Elfie was so taken aback that she didn't know what to say for a moment. Then she found her tongue. She had to get into the house somehow, even if it was to find that this was the wrong house.

'Sorry to bother you, ma'am. I'm looking for a Mrs Brown.'

'Mrs Brown?'

'Mrs Sadie Brown. She give me this address, said to call on her.'

'Are you sure, dear?' The woman had a kindly voice. Elfie relaxed a little. 'There's another Willow Tree Cottage in the district, so the postman told me.'

'I've just been there. It were the wrong one.'

'Oh dear. Have you come far?'

'London.'

'London! My goodness. That is a long way. Best come in for a minute.'

They went inside and the old lady led Elfie down the passage into a spotless kitchen. Brass pans hung around the walls.

'Sit yourself down, child. I was just making myself a

cup of tea. Would you like one?'

Elfie thought of that story about the witch in the wood feeding up Hansel and Gretel, but this old woman looked harmless, quite sweet, in fact. And she was so thin and small Elfie could knock her backwards if she had to.

'That'd be very nice. I got real thirsty walking along the road.'

'You didn't walk all the way from London surely?'

'No, no, just from Barnet, that's all.'

The tea was already made in a china pot, covered by a thick woolly cosy.

'My name's Kitty,' said Elfie.

'I'm Maisie. Maisie Mallow. But you can just call me Maisie. Sit yourself down, dear. It's nice for me to have a bit of company. It's not often anyone passes this way. Do you take milk? Sugar?

'Yes, please.'

'There you are, Kitty. Your friend, does she live in London?'

'Yes.'

'Which part would that be?'

Elfie thought quickly. 'Islington,' she said and then got a question in herself. 'Do you live alone then?'

'I have done this thirty years, since my poor husband died, God rest his soul.'

Elfie sipped her tea. It must be safe and wouldn't have had anything nasty like poison dropped into it since Maisie was drinking it too.

Elfie was truly puzzled. Could this really have been the house where Rosalind had been held by the kidnappers? Could this sweet old lady have been sitting down here in her kitchen drinking tea while Rosalind was held prisoner up in the attic? They'd read a number of stories in which people had turned out to be different from what they at first appeared. Or was there yet another Willow Tree Cottage? But this seemed like the right one, what with both the barn and the wood.

Elfie glanced up to see Joe's face at the window. Maisie fortunately had her back to him. Elfie made a little movement with her hand to signal that she was all right. Or, at least, she hoped she was.

'How do you manage, Maisie, away out here all on your own?'

'The tradesmen are very good. They bring everything I need. The milkman calls, the breadman, the grocery van. I don't want for anything.'

'That's good,' said Elfie. What else could she ask? She glanced round the room. There were two photographs on the shelf, one of an older man with a beard and a thick moustache, the other of a young child.

'Is that your husband?' Elfie indicated the man with the beard.

'That was Samuel, yes.'

'And the other one, is he your son?'

'No, we never had children of our own, dear. It's my nephew Stanley. He's the only family I have now. Very kind he is to me, too.'

'That's nice. Does he visit?'

'Once in a while. But a week or two back he gave me a very nice present indeed.' Maisie beamed. 'Very nice.'

'Oh,' said Elfie. This conversation didn't seem to be getting her anywhere. 'What kind of present did he give you?'

'A week at Southend-on-Sea. Can you imagine? I stayed in a lovely guest house, with all my meals provided. Very comfortable it was. Stanley took me there, brought me back, paid for the lot. Wasn't that good of him?'

'Very good of him.' Elfie couldn't help feeling quite excited. 'So when was that?'

'Oh I'm terrible with dates . . . I have it marked on the calendar there.' Maisie got up and fetched it. The dates were circled. And Elfie knew immediately that they coincided with the ones during which Rosalind had been held captive!

The shock was such that Elfie choked on her tea and started to splutter.

'Are you all right, dear?'

'I'm fine. Honest.'

'It was so lovely, being by the sea. You've no idea.' Maisie smiled at the recollection.

'That really was very nice of Stanley. It must have cost him quite a lot.'

'I was able to do something for him in return. Didn't cost me anything, though.'

'What was that?'

'I let him and his wife stay here for the week.'

'Here? In this very house?' Elfie's grin was enormous.

Maisie nodded. 'It gave them a chance to enjoy some country air. They could do with it, living as they do right in the middle of London, with all those smokey chimneys and terrible fogs.'

'So he's married, is Stanley?'

'Oh yes. Beryl's her name. They've been married for some years but they've no family. Beryl's all right, but not quite my kind of person, you know what I mean?'

Elfie nodded. She could hardly contain herself. Wait till she told Joe!

She got up and went over to take a closer look at Stanley's photo.

'He's quite handsome,' she commented, though he wasn't. He had a hard look around the eyes and then there was that downturned mouth.

'Do you think so, dear?' Maisie looked vague. He looks more like the other side.'

'So he's not called Mallow then?'

'No, dear, Stanley Watson is his name.'

'Whereabouts does he live in London?' Elfie tried to sound casual.

'The Mile End Road. That's in the East End, I believe? Never been there myself. Stanley says I wouldn't like it. Too busy. Too much traffic.'

'Why do they live in that part, then?'

'Work, of course.'

'What kind?'

'I've no idea about these things, dear.' Maisie was looking at Elfie thoughtfully. 'Some kind of garment-making business, I think.'

Joe was back at the window again. 'I must be getting along now, Maisie.'

'Oh, must you, dear? It's been lovely talking to you. Actually, Stanley and Beryl are due any minute. You could have waited and met them. I'd love you to have met him. Such a nice man. They're coming to pick up something that they left behind upstairs.'

'No, I would love to stay, but I must be on my way.' Elfie moved rapidly towards the door. 'Thanks for the tea, Maisie.'

'Pity you can't stop a while. Stanley might have been able to give you a lift back to the station. Save you a walk.'

'No, it's all right. I don't mind walking.'

Elfie was out in the hall now, with Maisie coming up behind her. Elfie opened the front door, trying not to look as if she was in a rush. She hoped Maisie couldn't hear her heart beating nineteen to the dozen.

'Thanks again, Maisie.'

'Any time, dear, if you're passing.'

Maisie waited at the door. Elfie turned at the end of the path to wave briefly before walking briskly on, knowing that Joe would follow. When she rounded a bend in the road she stopped to make sure she was out of sight of the cottage, and seconds later, Joe was beside her.

'Well, did you learn anything? You were in there long enough.'

'Learn anything? You're telling me I did!' But Elfie paused, holding her hand up, making Joe wait. 'Listen, can you hear wheels?'

Joe cocked his head. 'Yes, I can. Why, what's up?'

'They're coming.'

'Who's coming?'

'The kidnappers!'

Chapter Twelve:
Stanley and Beryl

Elfie and Joe dived into the wood without a moment to spare. A horse and trap carrying two passengers passed close to them. They saw the passengers clearly: a man wearing a checked flat cap and a woman in a black bonnet, a bit in the style of the Salvation Army hats. The man was stockily built and had a ruddy face while the woman had a pale, angular, sharp-chinned one. They were both hanging on for dear life as the driver urged the horse on. This was no relaxing Sunday outing to the country.

The cart rattled up to the front door of the cottage and jerked to a halt. The couple climbed out just as Maisie appeared on the doorstep. Joe pulled Elfie back. They had only a blurred view of the new arrivals through the trees but they could hear their voices clearly enough.

'Nice to see you, Auntie.'

'You too, Stanley. Aren't you coming in?'

'We can't stop, I'm afraid. We've got a train to catch back to London. Beryl can just nip upstairs and fetch the cloak.'

'Oh, very well.' Maisie sounded disappointed. 'I never go up to the attic myself with these creaky old knees, so I didn't notice it.'

'Best not to go up to the attic, Maisie. Those stairs are too steep for you. You might slip and damage yourself.'

'Did you happen to pass a young girl along the lane? She's on her way to the station. You might be able to give her a lift.'

'What girl?'

'She's called Kitty. Lovely child.'

'Kitty what?'

'She didn't tell me her second name.'

'What was she doing here?'

'She was looking for someone. A Mrs Brown. Sadie Brown? I couldn't help her but I brought her in and gave her a cup of tea and we had a lovely chat. I told her all about my lovely week in Southend. I did enjoy that, you know, Stanley.'

'You shouldn't be letting strangers come into your house.' Stanley's voice was sharp. 'They could take advantage of you, you being on your own. What did she look like, this girl?'

'She'd be about twelve years old. She had lovely dark curly hair and very big brown eyes.'

'We'll keep a look out.' There was the sound of heavy steps on the stairs.

'Did you find what you were looking for, Beryl?' asked Maisie as Stanley's wife walked out the front door.

'Yes, thanks.'

'That's pretty. Is it yours? Never seen you in that colour before.'

Elfie couldn't resist taking a peep and gasped. It was Rosalind's cornflower cloak that Beryl was holding over her arm. Her sister's favourite! Joe clamped a hand over Elfie's mouth before she could cry out.

'We'll see you soon, Maisie,' said Stanley. It was clear that he wanted to leave.

'I do hope so.'

'Ta, ta, then, Maisie,' said Beryl.

'Goodbye, Stanley. Goodbye, Beryl.'

Stanley and his wife climbed back into the trap, which wheeled about and came trundling down the path. They must have hired it at the station. It sounded as if it could come apart at any moment. The wheels passed once again within a foot of the two watchers and almost slid into the ditch. The passengers clung onto each other and Stanley swore.

'Watch what you're doing, man! You'll get us killed if you're not careful.'

The trap rattled out of sight and when the rumble of the wheels could no longer be heard Elfie and Joe emerged from the trees.

'So now we know who they are,' said Elfie.

'You got their names?'

'Of course! That's Maisie's nephew. He's called Stanley

Watson and she's called Beryl and they live in the Mile End Road.'

'You wouldn't happen to have got the number, I suppose?' Joe grinned as Elfie tried to land him a gentle punch but he sidestepped and avoided her, as always.

'No, you've done well, Elfie. Really well.'

They started back along the road towards Barnet, pausing at every corner in case the horse and trap might have broken down. They had to give the couple time to get to the station ahead of them, and on an earlier train to London, so they dallied a little. Elfie picked a small bunch of flowers by the wayside. The air was soft and balmy. It would have been a lovely day out if it hadn't been for the existence of Mr and Mrs Watson. And the fact that Rosalind was still separated from her parents.

Elfie and Joe ambled round a bend in the road and stopped in their tracks. There they were, Stanley and Beryl, in a ditch. Elfie had to stop herself laughing. The trap had overturned and the horse had broken free and was off galloping along the road. The driver was doing his best to haul his unfortunate passengers back onto their feet. They were cursing him loudly.

'Give us a hand then,' the carter called to Joe and Elfie.

'I'm not helping Rosalind's kidnappers,' muttered Elfie.

'Let's disappear.' Joe pulled Elfie back around the corner. Surely the Watsons hadn't had time to look them over? They had been too busy trying to struggle out of the ditch.

'You'll pay for this, my man,' Stanley Watson was shouting.

Beryl was angry too. 'Now what are we to do?'

Joe and Elfie took to their heels and ran. When they were well along the road they paused. There was no sound of the Watsons' voices.

'They'll have to leg it back to the station,' said Joe. 'Unless they manage to get a lift.'

They waited a while before they resumed their journey, walking past the abandoned trap looking forlorn in the ditch. The sun was moving round in the sky, the afternoon drawing in.

Elfie and Joe approached Barnet station with caution. There was no sign of the Watsons on the platform. The guard was announcing the arrival of the next train for London.

When the train pulled in it was already packed but Joe and Elfie managed to squeeze into a compartment. Neither spoke on the journey though they had plenty to think about.

ϡϡ

Saturday night at the *Pig and Whistle* was in full song by the time they arrived. Ma Bigsby was singing *Molly Malone*. Nobody had time to ask Elfie and Joe where they had been all day.

They were not so lucky the following morning. On Sundays Ma Bigsby took the twins with her to the Catholic chapel while Pa conducted the rest around a variety of churches of different faiths in rotation. He wanted them to be subjected to a variety of experiences, he said. This Sunday they went to the Salvation Army Hall, Elfie's favourite. She, like most of the children, loved the singing and the big sound of the trombones. The children were given tambourines to rattle and bang. The other churches seemed dull and sombre in comparison, though Pa insisted that some of the music was very fine.

'You have to learn to listen, Elfie,' he told her, again and again.

It was unfortunate, however, that it was the turn of the Salvation Army this particular Sunday. At the end of the service one of the trombone players rushed up to Elfie and Joe.

'We called out to you yesterday at the station, but you never heard us, you were that busy talking.'

Pa was standing nearby. 'Station?' He frowned. 'Which station was that?'

'King's Cross. We were playing a few hymns for the travellers. We thought Elfie and Joe might have liked to join us. Joe's got such a fine deep voice.'

'We were in a bit of a hurry.' Elfie avoided Pa's eye. The older children were given a generous amount of freedom, but that did not include going off on train journeys. Ma and Pa liked to know where they were at all times. More or less.

On the way home Pa let the other children run on ahead, allowing him to walk with Joe and Elfie.

'Here we go!' muttered Elfie to Joe. 'We ain't going to get away with it.'

'So what were you doing in King's Cross station last night, may I ask?' Pa never raised his voice, never got angry, but he could tick you off with a stern look.

'We went to Barnet,' said Joe, who believed that one should tell the truth or, at least, avoid telling a direct lie. Sometimes Elfie thought he went too far. 'I'm sorry, Pa,' Joe went on, 'we should have asked permission.'

'I would have preferred that you had. And what were you doing in Barnet?'

'We went walking in the countryside,' said Elfie. Well, that was the truth, wasn't it? 'Someone told us it was a lovely place, lots of fresh air. It was ever such a lovely day, wasn't it, Joe?'

'It was.'

They walked a little further before Pa spoke again. 'You do seem to be spending long hours away from the house these days. On Sundays, particularly. You are often gone for a while after lunch.'

'It's nice being outside in summertime,' said Elfie.

'Indeed it is. And where do you go on Sunday afternoons to enjoy the air?' He looked at Joe.

'Hampstead Heath.'

'It's a great place to walk.' Elfie jumped in quickly. 'There's always plenty of room. Rosalind and me used to fly kites there.'

'Rosalind and I,' said Pa. 'I take it you go there hoping for a sight of Rosalind? Am I right?'

'Well, yes,' admitted Elfie. There didn't seem any point in denying it.

'And have you ever seen her?'

'No.'

'Perhaps you are hoping for a miracle and that in some way Rosalind might be released.'

'Miracles do happen,' muttered Elfie. 'Bible says so.'

'True. But if if you think you can perform one yourselves and manage to rescue Rosalind you are making a mistake. Her grandfather, as you know, has total legal rights over her. Remember that. Hanging around Hampstead Heath might not be a good idea.'

They nodded. Pa let the matter drop then.

Later he eyed them both as they left the kitchen after lunch but made no comment, other than to warn them not to be late for supper.

∽✢∾

Lizzie was on time that Sunday.

'Lizzie,' began Joe, 'did Rosalind ever mention hearing the name Stanley while she was kept in that house in the country?' he asked.

'Stanley?' Lizzie thought, then shook her head. 'No.'

'Or Beryl?'

'Don't think she heard any names spoke at all. She didn't even see the woman's face when she brought her food.'

'Was she wearing her cornflower blue cloak when she was kidnapped?'

'Yes, she was! Her best, she said. She's mentioned that more than once. But it got left behind in the room when they took her away at the end. Can't tell you much more.'

They walked together in the sunshine before Lizzie left them to go and meet up with Kathleen. But before she went, they arranged to meet again the following Sunday.

Chapter Thirteen:
Mile End Road

Elfie was desperate to follow up their lead to the East End but she was forced to agree it would be difficult for them to go all the way out to Mile End and back after Joe finished work without raising Pa Bigsby's suspicions. It would have to wait until the following Saturday. Alfred Trelawney had decided not to open the office at all on Saturday mornings during the summer. His wife needed him by her side. She was a shadow of her former self, unable to come to terms with her father's cruel decision. She was continuing to come to the *Pig and Whistle* on weekdays but Saturdays were busy and Ma Bigsby had little time to spare.

So they had to wait for five whole days.

∽∾

Elfie hated the wait. She found it difficult to keep her mind on her work during lessons.

'Who did Queen Victoria succeed to the throne, Elfie?' asked Pa Bigsby one day. They were having a history lesson and normally Elfie enjoyed that.

Her head jerked up. She'd been trying to decide what they should wear on Saturday morning so that they would mingle with the kids in the East End. They'd need to look scruffy. There was a lot of poverty along there, she knew that only too well. She'd been part of it once herself. She'd been thinking that Joe would not stand out in the East End the way he did in Hampstead. A number of West Indians lived in that part of the city. They found work at the docks. Joe, she decided, would wear scuffed, short-legged pants and an old flat cap.

'Elfie, did you happen to hear me?' enquired Pa.

'Oh yes. Sorry, Pa. Queen Victoria . . .' Elfie racked her brains for some kind of answer. 'She died five months ago. I remember the day. Everyone was wearing black or purple. Mad Meg cried her eyes out.'

'Yes, we know that. But what I want to know is which monarch preceded her.'

Elfie stared at her desk. Her cheeks were flushed with embarrassment.

Ivy's hand shot up.

'You do know what preceded means, Elfie?' asked Pa.

'Came before.'

'Very good. So?'

'George somebody.'

'I'm afraid not.' He turned to Ivy. 'Well, Ivy?'

'William the Fourth.'

'You've been listening, Ivy.' Pa nodded with approval. 'And you, Elfie, have not.'

Elfie avoided Ivy's eye. She'd be smirking. Elfie didn't care. Let her! Wait till she and Joe found the kidnappers and got the money back for old Clarendon-Smythe, who would then be forced to give up Rosalind! But would he? Joe said he wouldn't like to lay a wager on it but they had to try anyway.

'I recommend, Elfie,' Pa continued, 'that you try to pay attention. It is possible that we may be receiving a visit from Mr Ramsbottom this morning.'

Everyone groaned.

The inspector did not turn up, however. They heard at lunchtime that he had tripped over a jagged paving stone and damaged his knee.

'What a piece of luck!' declared Elfie.

'Elfie!' Pa fixed her with a stare over the top of his monocle. But he was smiling

ᘛᘚ

On Saturday morning, after they had done their chores at the *Pig*, Joe and Elfie set off. When Ma saw them going out she said, 'What on earth have you got those old pants on for, Joe? They're halfway up your legs. You've grown like a beanpole this last year.'

'It's a warm day,' said Elfie, who was wearing a faded blue cotton dress and an old sun hat that had been put aside in the charity box.

They left before Ma could pass any more remarks on their clothing. Once they were out of sight Elfie took an old pinafore out of her bag and pulled it over her head.

They headed south, towards the river, keeping an eye open for carters. They knew a number who travelled this way regularly. Some went to the docks to pick up or drop off loads. Two or three passed by, and then one pulled his horse up to the curb beside them. His name was Eddie.

'Wotcha up to this morning then, you two?'

'We're wanting to go to the East End,' said Elfie.

'I'm goin' down to Limehouse. I could drop you off somewhere near.'

'That'd be wonderful, Eddie.'

'Won't be a comfortable ride, mind you.' He cast a look behind him. He was carrying scrap iron.

They jumped onto the back and clung on. Eddie was right about the comfort. By the time they were dropped off they each had a few scrapes on their arms and legs and their clothes looked as if they'd been dragged through a dust heap.

'All the better,' said Elfie cheerfully. 'We'll look more like the street kids now.'

They stood at the beginning of the Mile End Road and gazed along it. It was a long, broad, noisy street, busy with buses and carts, wagons and barrows, and the occasional cab or bicycle negotiating a path around them. People of all sizes, shapes and colours, thronged the pavements and spilled onto the roadway. Indians, Chinese, Malaysians mingled with the local East Enders.

Women pushed prams, some piled high with washing, while small children trailed along behind. Men lounged in doorways, smoking foul-smelling cigarettes. Others loitered on the pavement, ready to pick up dropped stubs or bits of orange or apple peel. Smallholders cried their wares. The oyster-seller was doing good trade.

Elfie liked all the hustle and noise.

'Where do we start in the middle of all this?' Joe looked around.

'I could ask in a shop,' suggested Elfie. 'What about that cobbler's over there? Everybody needs to get their shoes mended.'

The shop stank of old smelly shoes. An elderly man in a green apron had a boot upside down on a last and was working on the sole.

'Well?' he said, without looking up.

'I wonder if you'd know a Mr Stanley Watson? Or his wife Mrs Beryl Watson?'

'Why should I?'

'I thought they might come in to get their shoes mended?'

'Never heard of them.'

'Ta, anyway.' Elfie left as quickly as she could, and took a deep breath once she was outside again.

Joe was leaning against the wall outside, his cap tilted over his forehead. He could easily pass for a docker, thought Elfie, looking like that. He certainly seemed happier in a cap rather than the stiff bowler he wore to work.

They worked their way along the street, going in and out of the different shops. Greengrocers, pharmacists, sweet shops, bakers, laundries. Elfie did the talking while Joe kept watch on the street. Beryl might even be out doing her Saturday shopping. It wouldn't matter if they bumped into her. Neither she nor Stanley had had a good look at them.

'They must shop somewhere around here,' said Elfie desperately, after an hour had passed. They'd asked lots of people, but none of them had heard of the Watsons. 'They've got to eat, haven't they?'

They sat on a step for a while and watched the crowds coming and going. A girl stood on a corner selling matches. She looked sickly and tired. A man with one leg was selling balloons. Joe thought he might have been one of the soldiers who lost his leg in the Boer War.

Elfie rummaged in her bag and brought out a currant bun. She got up and went over to the match girl and laid it on her tray. The girl jumped nervously.

'Eat it!' said Elfie. 'It will do you good.'

The girl did not need to be told a second time.

As Elfie was going back to Joe, she heard her name being called.

'Elfie! Elfie, is that you?'

She looked round to see a woman wheeling a pram full of sheets with a small child perched on top.

'Jeannie!' Elfie ran over to give the woman a hug. Jeannie had been a good friend to her, had given her the odd bun and mug of tea in the past when she'd been starving. Jeannie lived in a street off the Mile End Road, she remembered.

'Haven't seen you in ages, luv. Where you bin this last while?' asked Jeannie. 'My, you've grown. You're looking well too.'

'It's a long story, Jeannie. I don't sleep out any more.'

'Come on home with me and tell me what you've been up to. We can have a jar of tea together.'

Elfie signalled to Joe to join them.

'This is my friend, Joe. Joe, this is Jeannie.'

Jeannie lived in a small, two-roomed terraced house with her husband and seven children. He worked at the East India Dock.

'It's a right muddle in here,' said Jeannie apologetically.

'We don't notice muddles,' said Elfie.

There was little spare room in the house so they went outside and sat on the front step to drink their tea. Several of Jeannie's children were playing on the pavement. One was bowling a hoop. Another had made a bogie out of an old soap box with a couple of rusted pram wheels.

Elfie told Jeannie about the *Pig and Whistle* and Ma and Pa Bigsby and Jeannie shook her head in astonishment.

'My, were you not the lucky one!'

Jeannie herself had never had much luck. Her life was hard. She had a terrible racking cough and was as thin as a matchstick.

'So what brought the two of you down here today?' she asked.

'We're looking for a couple of people. Their name's Watson. He's called Stanley and she's Beryl.'

'Them two!' Jeannie made a face.

'Do you know them?'

'They have the pawnshop further up Mile End.'

'That'll be them!' said Elfie.

'What do you know about them?' asked Joe.

'I've been in the shop a few times over the years but now I've nothing left to pawn. They drive a hard bargain, let me tell you. They can be nasty too.'

Joe looked thoughtful. Elfie knew what would be going through his head since it was going through hers too. How could a pair of East End pawnbrokers organise such a big crime as a kidnapping? That took money, more than could be made from squeezing money out of people like Jeannie. It also took brains.

'Is he a well-built sort of fellow?' asked Joe. 'With a ruddy face?'

'Jowly chin,' added Elfie. 'Looks like a pug.'

'That's him all right,' confirmed Jeannie, laughing.

'Are they well off? I mean, do they seem to be rolling in money?'

'They've got more than you'd think, looking at their shop. I've heard tell that deals go on through the back.' Jeannie shrugged. 'Well, you know how it is at the docks, Elfie. A lot of thieving goes on. But I believe they're into bigger stuff. Why do you want to know about them? Doesn't sound as if you've much need of a pawnbroker's these days.'

'We can't tell you, I'm afraid.' Elfie dropped her voice. 'And don't let on to anyone that we were asking about them, Jeannie. All right?'

'All right with me. I can keep my mouth shut. I wouldn't want to get on the wrong side of them two anyway.'

The baby in the pram began to scream so Jeannie lifted him out.

'We'd best be getting on our way,' said Elfie. 'It's been lovely seeing you though, Jeannie.'

'Thanks very much for the tea,' said Joe.

'Come back again and see me. It's been a real tonic.'

'We will,' promised Elfie.

Joe gave a sixpence to the eldest boy and told him to buy sweets for himself and the other children.

Their next stop was the pawnbroker's.

Chapter Fourteen:
At the Pawnbroker's

The street was even busier by now.

Elfie stopped abruptly. 'Oh no!' she cried, and pulled Joe into a doorway.

'What's up?' he asked .

'See, over there!' Elfie pointed across the street. 'Gertie. Dirty Gertie!'

Gertie was one of Elfie's old enemies from her time on the street. Gertie had once persuaded Ma Bigsby to take her in but she hadn't lasted long. Life in the *Pig* hadn't suited her. There had been too many rules and she didn't want lessons about history or anything else, so she'd skipped off one morning early, taking clothes and all sorts of other things away with her. Elfie had been flaming.

Gertie was begging in a doorway.

'Just keep going,' warned Joe. 'You don't want to tangle with her.'

'But she stole from Ma!' The thought of it still made Elfie feel furious.

'We're not going to do anything about that now. Keep going!' Joe prodded Elfie on. 'We've got to find the pawnbroker's.'

'I see it! Look, on the corner over there.'

The three golden balls of the pawnbroker's sign hung over the doorway, gleaming in the sunshine.

'Let's cross the road.' Joe took Elfie's hand.

They dodged through the traffic and stopped a few yards short of the pawnbroker's. They had not worked out a plan of campaign for this next step.

They considered their options.

'What do we do now?' Elfie wiped her sweaty palms on her pinafore.

'We can't just walk in there and look round,' said Joe.

'I could go in,' offered Elfie. 'I've been in plenty of pawnshops before.'

'What would you say?'

'That I'm looking for my auntie and that she'd said she was bringing in something to pawn.'

Joe looked doubtful.

'We can't just stand here,' complained Elfie, impatient as ever. 'And it'd be easier for me to go in than you.'

Joe conceded that. 'All right, give it a try. But for goodness' sake don't say your auntie's called Sadie Brown!'

Elfie was glad he'd mentioned that for she might just have done it without thinking. She pulled her sun hat further down over her face, walked up to the pawnshop door and pushed it open. It was like all the other pawnshops she'd seen in poor parts of the town, filled with cheap rubbish mostly, apart from a glass case which had jewellery and watches locked inside it. Whether the silver was real or not was another matter.

On the floor, on shelves, lay manky blankets and quilts, boots and shoes that had seen better days, bits of crockery and teapots, well-used prams, chipped china dolls, an odd-shaped trumpet and a set of bashed drums, well-worn leather belts and women's handbags, a frayed feather boa and a mangy fox-fur stole with a gleaming beady black eye. There were also books, magazines, wall clocks, mantelpiece clocks, sets of cutlery, beer mugs, christening mugs, babies' cradles. Everything was covered with a layer of dust and looked as if it had lain there for a very long time.

And then something caught Elfie's eye. It was all she could do to stop herself from crying out. Rosalind's cornflower blue cloak was lying over the back of a chair!

'What are you after?' demanded a sharp female voice.

Elfie whirled round to find herself eye to eye with Beryl.

'Light-fingered, are you? Well, you'd best keep them off my stuff or it'll be the worse for you.'

'I was looking for my auntie.' Elfie tried to sound indignant.

'Well, she ain't here. There's nobody here. You can see that for yourself, can't you? You've got eyes in your head.'

'My auntie said she was bringing in a brooch. It's got a lovely blue stone set in it.'

'Probably glass.' Beryl was standing so close that Elfie could feel her breath on her face and she didn't like it. She took a step to the side.

'So, what's your auntie's name?'

'Florrie.' It was the first name to pop into Elfie's head. There must be dozens of Florries in London and their very own Florrie would never come down here.

'Florrie what?'

'Dickens.' Pa Bigsby was reading *Oliver Twist* to them.

'Florrie Dickens? Never 'eard of her.'

'Beryl,' called a voice from the back. 'Come here a minute. We've got a visitor.'

'I'm coming, Stan. Hang on there a minute. I've got a bit of trash to get rid of first.'

Elfie was tempted to thump Beryl but resisted.

Beryl turned Elfie round and marched her to the door. 'Don't bother your head coming in here again! You might just get those light fingers of yours trampled on.'

'I didn't come in here to nick anything,' Elfie said hotly. 'I was just looking for . . .'

'Oh yes, for your Auntie Florrie. Think I was born yesterday? I'm not that daft.'

Beryl shoved Elfie in the back out onto the pavement and slammed the door shut behind her.

Elfie stood on the pavement raging. She'd get Beryl for that!

'Are you all right?' Joe joined her. They moved away from the door.

'It's the kidnappers' shop right enough,' Elfie told him. 'You wouldn't believe it but Rosalind's cloak was there! Can you imagine? Lying over a chair.'

'That's a mistake on their part,' observed Joe. 'Keeping it. It could be used as evidence against them.'

'It could? We can nail them then.'

'They'd probably claim someone brought it in. It wouldn't prove anything, not in itself. I still can't help wondering if they really could have organised the whole kidnapping on their own.'

'They don't look as if they've come into money.' Joe was mulling things over.

'There's Willow Tree Cottage too,' said Elfie. 'Rosalind could vouch for that.'

'She's locked up, remember?'

'But if we had enough evidence the police could take her there, couldn't they?'

'We'd need a bit more to convince the police. And Rosalind's grandfather. Let's take a walk round the corner and see if we can get along the back.'

A lane ran behind the shop. The gate of the pawnbroker's backyard was closed. Elfie was going to try the handle but Joe shook his head. They walked on.

They'd gone only a few yards when they heard the gate creak open behind them.

'Duck!' ordered Joe, pulling Elfie down with him behind an overflowing refuse bin.

'I'll sort that out later.' It was a man's voice. They'd heard that voice before. 'Don't worry, Stan, I'll be back and I'll see you're all right.' Footsteps led away from where they were hidden.

They peered over the top of the bin.

'It's Dimmock,' gasped Elfie.

'Come on, let's follow him,' said Joe.

Elfie brushed some filthy potato peelings and various other things off her pinafore and followed Joe along the alley. She stank. She looked and smelt like a real street kid now.

Turning into the main road they saw Dimmock's head bobbing along in amongst the crowd. He was a tall man, well over six feet.

'He seems to be making for the bus stop,' said Joe. 'Let's see if we can sneak on the bus after him.'

'Oi, oi,' came a voice from the doorway. 'If it ain't our Elf. Come down in the world again, have yez? Did yer get the boot? I see ye've still got yer darkie with yez.'

It was Gertie, of course. Who else?

Elfie confronted her. 'You shut your gob!' She was getting worked up, wagging her finger in the girl's face.

Joe pulled her back. 'Leave it, Elfie. It's not worth it. Anyway, here's a bus coming.'

Elfie turned to see a light-green bus pulling into the stop. A number 1. It was going to Oxford Circus.

'Rubbish!' Elfie snapped at Gertie.

As she moved away, Gertie spat, hitting Elfie on the cheek.

'You . . . !' For once in her life Elfie was lost for words.

Joe yanked her on, wondering what she might come out with when she found them. Elfie, still spluttering with fury, wiped her cheek with the skirt of her pinafore, then pulled it over her head and threw it in a bin.

'Get a move on!' urged Joe.

The bus was filling up. Dimmock had already boarded and gone upstairs.

'Standing room only,' called the conductor. 'Move along there now.'

Joe paid and they pushed their way through to the back. The bus smelt, too, of packed, sweaty human bodies. They missed the garden seats up top, their favourites, in the fresh air. Elfie felt sick.

The bus lurched its way along, heading westward, halting at every stop to let people off and on. Joe kept his eye fixed on the stair, watching in case Dimmock came down and jumped off quickly. He might not be going as far as Oxford Street.

Joe was right. Dimmock was getting off at Holborn, near the corner of Gray's Inn Road. Joe grabbed Elfie's hand and towed her behind him through the standing passengers.

'Mind where ye're goin'.' One woman was annoyed. 'You just stood on my foot.'

'Sorry,' said Elfie. 'Didn't mean to.'

By the time they landed on the pavement Dimmock had already started up Gray's Inn Road. It was a long walk on a warm day. Dimmock stepped out with a long stride, as did Joe, whereas Elfie was forced to break into a run at times to keep up.

'He's fit,' commented Joe. 'Looks like he could have been a boxer.'

Dimmock turned off on a side street before reaching St Pancras Station. Joe held Elfie back at the corner while he peered round.

'He's going into a building. It's all right, he's gone. Let's walk past and see what it is.'

It was only a few yards along the street. A brass plate on the door bore the name *Bertrand C. Grimble, Solicitor-at-Law.*

Chapter Fifteen:
Bertrand C. Grimble

'Crikey!' exclaimed Elfie. 'Greasy old Grimble.'

'Interesting,' said Joe. 'Very interesting. But we'd better move on in case Dimmock's making only a quick call. He'd definitely remember us.'

They retraced their steps to the corner and walked the rest of the way up to Euston Road.

'I could do with a cuppa,' sighed Elfie. 'I'm parched. There's the Euston Road Cocoa Rooms we could go to?' She looked at Joe, hopeful.

'Let's do that.'

They sat at a table by the window.

'That don't half feel good,' said Elfie, after she'd taken a long drink of tea from her mug. 'Almost as good as Ma's.' The tea had revived her curiosity. 'So what do you think Dimmock's up to with Greasy Grimble?'

'I'm just wondering about that myself. He could be bringing a message from Clarendon-Smythe, of course.

But then, what does Dimmock have to do with Stanley and Beryl? What was he up to in the pawnbroker's?'

Both of them paused to sip their tea. It had been a long morning.

'I just don't get it,' said Elfie. 'It's a bit of a coincidence, him knowing Stanley and Beryl, isn't it?'

'Is it?' Joe's eyes met Elfie's and suddenly she clutched his hand.

'Dimmock could have been involved in the kidnapping.' The idea excited Elfie. 'Why else was he there? He'd know all about Rosalind's movements, wouldn't he? Where she went to school, what time she got out.'

'I suppose he could have been the one to tip them off. Or even set it up.'

'And Greasy Grimble?'

'Well, he could have been in on it as well. He looks shady enough. I can't believe that the Watsons would have been able to organise the whole thing themselves.'

'What a turn up for the book it'd be if old Clarendon-Smythe found that his butler and his lawyer had done it! He might have a heart attack,' Elfie added hopefully.

'If we could prove that Dimmock and Grimble were involved it might just make him change his mind about Rosalind.'

'It'd take the wind out of his sails, wouldn't it?'

Joe said they must consider the evidence they could present to the police.

'Couldn't we just carry on ourselves?'

'How could we? We can't arrest them.'

Elfie didn't like the idea of the police coming in and pushing them aside and taking all the credit for themselves. Not that Dowdy would be like that but Sergeant Feather would probably want to call in Scotland Yard. It made him feel important when he did.

'We've got to think it through.' Joe was still pondering. 'I mean, what evidence do we really have? A lot of it's guesswork.'

'There's Willow Tree Cottage,' Elfie reminded him.

'I know. Rosalind should be able to identify the attic from what Lizzie has told us.'

'And Maisie can tell the police how she was away that week and Stanley and Beryl came to stay there.' Elfie was getting worked up again. She could hardly stay in her chair. 'The calendar's marked. And then there's Rosalind's cloak in the pawnshop.'

'Let's hope they don't sell it first.'

'It had a label on it saying five shillings. Five shillings! Nobody's going to pay that for a cloak along there.'

'Then there's Dimmock,' said Joe slowly. 'We don't have any real evidence against him.'

'We can tell the police we saw him coming out of the back entrance of the shop.'

'Our word against his.'

'But Stanley and Beryl will spill the beans on him if they get arrested.' Elfie felt sure about that. Joe might be training to be a lawyer, but she had seen more crimes going on right under her nose during her time living on the streets.

'I think you're probably right. They're not going to take the blame for Dimmock.'

'Then there's Greasy Grimble.'

Joe and Elfie made their way back to the *Pig*, their heads full of what they had discovered.

৩৩

As they were finishing their Sunday lunch, Pa said, 'Will you be going to Hampstead Heath this afternoon then, Elfie?'

'We might,' muttered Elfie, not meeting him in the eye.

'I take that to be a "yes"?'

'We had thought of going,' admitted Joe.

'I was thinking you might take Dora and Nancy with you,' continued Pa. 'You'd like a chance to go and visit Hampstead Heath, wouldn't you, girls?'

'Oh yes, Pa, we would!'

Elfie looked at Joe. This would complicate matters for them.

'It costs a lot for bus fares,' she said.

'You and Joe always seem to find the money.'

'Joe has his wages.'

'And I will pay for Nancy and Dora'.

'What about me?' demanded Ivy.

'I thought you and Mabel might take the little ones to the park. You may each have an ice cream.' That softened Ivy. Pa turned to Billy. 'I expect you've got your own plans?'

'He'll be going to the railway station *again*,' said Ivy. 'You'd think he'd seen enough trains.'

But everyone knew Billy could never see enough trains.

There was no question of going against Pa Bigsby's wishes, not when he spoke so decidedly. Elfie and Joe would take the twins to Hampstead Heath whether it was convenient or not.

The girls chattered excitedly while they waited for a bus to take them into town.

'What are we going to do about Lizzie?' Elfie asked Joe.

'You can go and meet her and I will stay with the twins.'

The buses were slow and less frequent on Sundays and they had to change three times. They arrived at the heath at five minutes past three.

'You'd better run,' said Joe. He'd brought a bat and ball with him. 'I'll play with the twins.'

The girls loved Joe and were happy to stay with him.

Elfie ran all the way to the lane and was out of breath when she reached Lizzie who was leaning against the wall, looking forlorn.

'Oh, Elfie, I was beginning to wonder if you'd come.'

'Sorry I'm late, Lizzie.' Elfie caught her breath. 'How's Rosalind been this week?'

'Crying her eyes out still. It makes my heart bleed to see her, so it does. She's so lonely, poor child.'

Elfie thought of Stanley and Beryl, Dimmock and

Grimble, and anger flared inside her. She was more determined than ever to catch the whole lot of them and free Rosalind! Joe kept reminding her that, even if they did, Clarendon-Smythe might still not give Rosalind up. But surely he would! He'd get his money back – if the gang hadn't spent it, of coursewillow and that might soften his heart. Clarissa said the only two things her father cared about in life were money and keeping his position in society.

'Has Rosalind remembered anything else, Lizzie?'

'Matter of fact, she has. Two things. She told me she tried to fly her handkerchief out of the skylight window but it got stuck and the window closed on it. She said the hanky was still there, hanging half in and half out. It was one her Papa had given her, too.'

Elfie was delighted. It could be yet another bit of evidence!

'Which of her handkerchiefs was it?' Elfie asked.

'It had roses embroidered on it and her initial R.'

'That's great. And the other thing?'

'A ribbon, a pink ribbon. She tucked it under the mattress, she said. It was one of her best and she didn't want it taken away.'

'This is wonderful,' said Elfie. 'Just wait till I tell Joe.'

'Does it help?' Lizzie sounded dubious.

'It might.'

Suddenly, they heard a roar, and whirling round they saw Dimmock charging towards them like an angry bull.

He seized Lizzie by the shoulder and when Elfie tried to intervene he shoved her aside so that she staggered and fell onto one knee. She scrambled up at once.

'What are you doing talking to this girl?' Dimmock demanded of Lizzie, who was trembling with fright.

'Why shouldn't she talk to me?' countered Elfie.

'Stay out of the way, you, and mind your own business! Go on, scram!'

'It is my business. And I ain't scarpering nowhere.'

He ignored her and shook Lizzie again.

'I want to know what you were talking to this girl about?'

'You're hurtin' me!'

'I'll hurt you some more if you don't tell me!' He raised his hand.

'Don't you dare!' cried Elfie and then realised straightaway that interference from her might have been a mistake. It was.

Dimmock slapped Lizzie hard across the cheek. 'Were you talking about Mr Clarendon-Smythe's private affairs?'

'I don't know nothing about his private affairs,' sobbed Lizzie. 'Honest I don't.'

'You're always talking to the young girl in the house, aren't you? I've seen you whispering in corners together.'

'If you mean Rosalind, why don't you say so?' broke in Elfie. 'We all know she's in there.'

'You shut up, you little brat, or I'll sort you out once and for all!'

Dimmock shook Lizzie again. 'So . . . tell me. What were you talking about?'

'All right,' said Elfie. Lizzie was crying uncontrollably. He wasn't going to get any answers from her. 'I'll tell you. I was just checking Rosalind was all right. Doesn't sound like she is when she's shut up like a prisoner in that nasty old dungeon of a house with people like you.'

Dimmock pushed Lizzie away from him. 'You are dismissed from Mr Clarendon-Smythe's employ, as from this moment. You will come with me and collect your belongings and leave forthwith.'

'You can't do that to her,' protested Elfie.

'Oh yes, I can! I run the household for Mr Clarendon-Smythe.'

'Bully!' Elfie stepped out of his reach.

He grabbed Lizzie's arm and marched her back along the street towards the house. Elfie followed. Lizzie wept the whole way. Elfie called out to her not to worry, she'd see she wouldn't have to sleep on the street.

Dimmock took Lizzie in by the back gate, slamming it shut in Elfie's face. It took no more than ten minutes for Lizzie to pack her belongings. Dimmock pushed her out through the gate into the lane where Elfie was waiting. Lizzie was trembling from head to foot. The gate slammed shut behind her and the bolt was rammed shut.

'Don't worry, Lizzie,' Elfie told her again. 'We'll see you're all right.'

But now, she realised, Rosalind had lost the only

friend she had in the house and Elfie couldn't help but worry about that.

Chapter Sixteen:
Lizzie Homeless

Elfie and Joe took Lizzie home with them. They had to. They couldn't leave her standing on the heath clutching her bag. Besides, it was due to them that she had lost her job.

'Why's she coming with us?' asked Nancy, as they trudged back towards the main road.

'Because she's got nowhere to stay,' said Elfie.

The twins weren't happy at being dragged away from the heath so quickly. They'd had hardly any time to play. They grumped and dragged their feet.

'I'm just being a nuisance,' wailed Lizzie.

'No, you're not,' said Joe. 'It's our fault.'

'Ma Bigsby's very nice,' Elfie reassured Lizzie. 'You'll like her. Everybody does. She won't turn you away.'

Ma would not turn Lizzie away but she would not be overjoyed, either. There was no room for another adult in the house. They were packed in like sardines as it was.

The twins continued to grizzle all the way home. Lizzie couldn't stop crying.

They had a lot of explaining to do when they arrived back at the *Pig and Whistle*. Ma, as expected, welcomed Lizzie, told her to sit down in the comfy chair in the kitchen and made her a nice cup of tea.

'I'm real sorry.' Lizzie was trembling.

'Don't you bother your head, girl. You're most welcome in our house. Besides, you're from the old country.'

That made Lizzie smile a little.

Pa asked Elfie and Joe to join them in his study.

'So this young lady works for Mr Clarendon-Smythe?'

'She did,' answered Joe. 'Until today.'

'And how did you come to be acquainted with her?'

'It was like this,' began Elfie, but was interrupted by Pa.

'I think perhaps Joe might tell me.'

'We met her coming out of the Clarendon-Smythe house one Sunday.'

'So you accosted her?'

'Well, we spoke to her.' Joe was uncomfortable.

Elfie could not keep quiet. 'We knew Rosalind liked her so we sort of asked her a few questions.'

'Such as?'

'How Rosalind was, things like that.'

'And what did you learn?'

'That Rosalind was unhappy. It's awful, Pa! She cries her eyes out from morning till night.'

'I am not surprised to hear that. Poor child. And this afternoon? What happened then?'

Joe told him how Dimmock had found Lizzie talking to Elfie and sacked her. It seemed better for him to explain as Elfie could not even think about it without her blood starting to boil.

'I see.' Pa put the tips of his fingers together and examined them. 'Has any of this helped to further the cause of Rosalind at all?'

Elfie longed to tell him about Willow Tree Cottage and how she'd seen Rosalind's cloak lying over the chair in the pawnshop in the Mile End Road but she and Joe had agreed to say nothing until they had put their case together. Those had been his words. Joe was getting more lawyer-like every day. Elfie's father was teaching him well. She hadn't had time yet to tell him about the handkerchief stuck in the attic window of Willow Tree Cottage, or the ribbon under the mattress.

'I'm going to ask. In fact, I'm going to order the two of you to stay away from Hampstead Heath and the Clarendon-Smythes' house.' Pa regarded each of them in turn with his piercing blue eyes. 'Understand?'

Joe nodded.

'Elfie?'

'Yes, Pa.'

When they went downstairs Ma said she was going out for a few minutes. She took off the wide canvas apron that she wore wrapped around her middle from morning till night and put on her Sunday-going-to-church coat.

'You might start to get supper organised, Elfie.'

'Yes, Ma,' said Elfie meekly.

She laid the table, taking care to line up the knives and forks. Ma was particular about things like that. Elfie was dying to tell Joe about Rosalind's handkerchief but there were too many people around. Lizzie sat in the chair clutching her bag and continuing to weep at intervals into a large handkerchief that Ma had given her. Elfie kept telling her not to worry. They'd sort something out.

When Ivy returned with Mabel and the younger children she bragged about having had an ice cream and how the man had given her an extra dollop and extra raspberry syrup on top.

'We didn't get an ice cream,' complained Dora.

'You should have come with us,' retorted Ivy.

Ma came back in less than an hour, took off her coat, hung it up in the cupboard and wrapped her apron round her body again.

'Come with me for a moment, Lizzie,' she said. 'We'll go into the bar.'

The pub didn't open on Sundays so they had the place to themselves. Elfie followed. Joe was in there polishing the brasses. They were in need of it after a Saturday night.

'I've just been talking to a Mrs Walkingshaw,' Ma began and Elfie's spirits lifted. 'She lives in a very nice house up past the park and she's looking for a live-in-general. She asked Florrie to keep an ear open. She's a lovely woman, Mrs Walkingshaw, a widow woman, and her only son lives up in Yorkshire. She'd treat you well, Lizzie, I would swear on that. You can think it over if you like.'

Lizzie didn't need time to think it over. She accepted straightaway.

'Thank you so much, Mrs Bigsby.'

'Just call me Ma. Everybody does, the customers and all.'

'I'm ever so grateful,' Lizzie went on. 'I 'ated that house! They'd give you the creeps, they would, Mr and Mrs Dimmock. And then there's the manservant Quirk. They're right thick with 'im. He's always creepin' about the place, watchin' us, spyin' on us.'

Elfie decided to remember that name. You never knew when something like that would come in useful. She was learning that from Joe.

They were both relieved that Ma had found a place for Lizzie. She was good at sorting things out, was Ma. Elfie's spirits dropped again, though, as soon as she thought of her poor sister, friendless, in that house.

'We'll keep you with us tonight, Lizzie,' said Ma. 'You can share Elfie's mattress. You're both skinny as rakes. Yet Elfie eats like a horse!'

'Ma!' complained Elfie.

Ma ignored her. 'I'll take you up to see Mrs Walkingshaw in the morning after breakfast, Lizzie.'

Elfie thought she might go with her – after all she still felt responsible for Lizzie losing her last job.

And so it was. Ma, dressed once more in her good coat, walked between the two girls. Lizzie and Mrs Walkingshaw took to each other at once.

'All's well that ends well,' declared Ma on the way home. It was not often she quoted Shakespeare. Seldom, in fact. Pa, of course, was different.

All might be ending well for Lizzie, thought Elfie, but it hadn't ended for Rosalind yet. They would have to renew their efforts. Rosalind could not be allowed to stay locked up in that house on the heath much longer.

⁘

After lessons that Tuesday, Elfie had to do some deliveries for the pharmacist. One of them took her up past the park, near Mrs Walkingshaw's house. She rang the bell and Lizzie came to the door, wearing a black dress and white apron and cap.

'Oh, Elfie!' she cried, giving her hug. 'Are you comin' in?'

'No, I can't stop, Lizzie. I'm in a right hurry. I've got to go down to my papa's office to see Joe. I just called in to see if you were all right.'

'Oh, I am, certainly I am! What a bit of luck, me meeting you and Joe!'

Elfie left her, feeling happy about that, at least. She'd just finished her round when Tommy pulled his cart up beside her, asking if she was going anywhere. He could take her down to Euston Road. She leapt on board.

'Where's your mate today?'

'Waiting for me in the office.'

She found Joe sitting alone at his desk looking gloomy.

'Where's Papa?' asked Elfie.

'He's gone to the Inns of Court with a client.'

'That's good. What you looking so morose for then?'

Pa Bigsby had been telling them only that morning that morose was another word for gloomy. He was keen that they should extend their vocabulary, as he put it.

Joe grinned and his face lightened for a moment, then darkened again.

'What's up?'

'Look!' He pointed to a copy of the *Daily Express* lying spread open on the desk.

Elfie leant over his shoulder and read:

FIRE AT MILE END

Fire at well-known pawnbroker's on the Mile End Road.

Two dead.

Arson suspected.

Chapter Seventeen: The Fire at Mile End

They went to see for themselves. The pawnbroker's shop was completely gutted. Wisps of smoke still rose from the jagged pile. *Underneath it must lie Rosalind's cloak*, thought Elfie. A group of people stood around, shaking their heads and marvelling at the sight.

'Went up with a bang it did,' said an elderly woman. 'I was on the other side of the road, praise the Lord!'

'Good riddance is what I say,' said the elderly man beside her.

'Now, Albert, that's not a very nice thing to say about the dead.'

Elfie shuffled into the circle. 'They didn't seem terribly nice. The pawnbroker and his wife? At least from what I've heard.'

'They weren't popular, I'll give you that,' agreed the woman.

'Popular!' snorted her husband. 'Couple of crooks.'

'Did the police never catch them at anything then?' Elfie was going to get in as many questions as she could.

'Too smart, they were. Knew how to cover their backs.'

'What time did it happen? The fire?'

'Must have been getting on for midnight. We were coming back from visiting the wife's sister.'

'Anyone got any idea who did it?'

Elfie and Joe looked at each other.

'There must be a good few who wouldn't have minded chucking in a can of paraffin.'

'Our Johnnie saw a man in the back lane about that time,' another woman put in. 'He was carrying something. We told the police but Johnnie couldn't give much of a description, except to say that he was a big fellow.'

Elfie looked round, sensing someone behind her. It was Gertie.

'What you doing here?' asked Elfie. Gertie was the last person she wanted to see.

'I seen the man.' Gertie sounded pleased with herself.

'Honest? The one what did it?' Immediately Elfie put her dislike to one side. This could be important.

Gertie nodded.

'What did he look like?' asked Joe.

'He'd a big boxer's nose on him. I'd seen him goin' in there before. Always went by the back lane.'

'You should tell the police,' said Joe.

'Me, tell the police! You've got to be jokin'.' Even as she said it, Gertie slid away into the crowd.

Joe and Elfie moved away too.

'So do you think it was Dimmock?' asked Elfie.

'Sounds like him. When we saw him earlier he said he'd be back.'

'To sort things out!'

'So he's now got rid of our two main suspects, who could grass on him. No doubt that was why he did it. If he did it. This is all supposition, you know.'

'Of course he did it!' protested Elfie.

Joe could be annoying at times, always questioning things, wanting to be absolutely, completely sure.

'So Dimmock will think he's in the clear now,' said Elfie.

'We can't *prove* anything against him.'

'And what about Greasy Grimble?'

'Same goes for him. Rosalind's cloak's gone up in smoke too. We've still not got much hard evidence.'

That reminded Elfie to tell Joe about the handkerchief and the pink ribbon. 'We could tell the police to go and see if they can find them at Willow Tree Cottage.'

'We could try.' Joe was looking uneasy. 'I'm worried in case Dimmock might go after Lizzie. We know he'll stop at nothing. He might suspect she's told us something.'

Joe had enough money left for them to go home by bus. But instead of getting off at the usual stop, they carried on further up Green Lanes.

'They'll be eating,' said Elfie, as they passed the *Pig and Whistle*.

'We can't help it.'

When they reached Mrs Walkingshaw's they banged the brass door knocker and waited. They heard movement inside the house but the door didn't open.

'Who is it?' Lizzie's voice emerged through the slit of the letter box.

'It's us. Elfie and Joe.'

Lizzie opened the door.

'Who is it, Lizzie?' Mrs Walkingshaw called from the back of the house.

'It's all right, Mrs Walkingshaw. It's me friends, Elfie and Joe.'

'Invite them in then, girl.'

Mrs Walkingshaw came into the hall and shook hands with them. She was elderly but sprightly. She had met Elfie before, of course, but not Joe. The sight of him threw her for a moment but she rallied and was courteous, saying that she was very pleased to meet him. Especially after their earlier caller.

'A most unpleasant man,' she told them. 'Lizzie had gone to buy some provisions so I answered the door to him myself.'

'It was Dimmock,' said Lizzie.

Joe nodded.

'Very demanding he was too,' continued Mrs Walkingshaw. 'His behaviour was quite threatening. He tried to tell me that Lizzie was a liar and a thief and I should not employ her.'

'That's not true!' exploded Elfie.

'No, it ain't,' cried Lizzie.

'He's the liar,' said Joe quietly.

'I could believe that. He had the nerve to put his foot over my doorstep. I told him I would call the police if he did not leave immediately. He could see that I was not to be trifled with so he left.'

'Good for you, Mrs Walkingshaw,' said Elfie.

'How would he know where I was?' asked Lizzie anxiously.

'He must know where Elfie and I live . . . maybe from Rosalind or her grandfather,' replied Joe. 'Then came snooping round the *Pig*.'

'He could have asked someone if they'd seen you,' suggested Elfie. 'We'll have to investigate.'

Joe told Lizzie she'd been right not to answer the door without asking who it was. 'And Mrs Walkingshaw, if he does come back, please do phone the police.'

'Ask for Dowdy,' added Elfie. 'Constable O'Dowd. He's a great bobby and a good friend of ours.'

'We shall do that.'

Elfie and Joe ran all the way back to the *Pig*. The children were playing on the pavement outside. The boys were rolling marbles and the girls had tied a rope to a lamppost and were skipping back and forth.

Elfie jumped in.

'Hey!' cried Ivy, who was coiling the rope.

Elfie carried on and sang as she skipped.

Do you know last night and the night before,
Three tomcats came knocking at my door,
One had a fiddle, one had a drum

And one had a pancake stuck to its bum!'

'That's rude,' said Ivy. As if she couldn't be rude herself! Joe was laughing.

'You missed your dinner,' said Ivy.

'No need to tell us,' retorted Elfie.

'Did a man come round here earlier, Ivy?' asked Joe. 'A stranger? Big fellow. Asking about Lizzie.'

'He were here before dinner, matter of fact,' said Ivy. 'Looking for Lizzie. Said she was his sister.'

'What a liar!' said Elfie.

'Ivy, did you tell him anything?' asked Joe.

Ivy was looking nervous. 'Just that she'd gone to work for Mrs Walkingshaw up by the park.'

'You shouldn't have done that,' snapped Elfie. 'He's a crook.'

'How were I to know?'

'*Was*,' said Elfie.

'Not your fault, Ivy,' said Joe.

Ivy stuck out her tongue at Elfie.

Joe and Elfie went inside to 'face the music'. It was one of Ma's own phrases, though she wasn't singing now. No strains of *Molly Malone* or *The Rose of Tralee* issued from the kitchen. Ma was cross. She told them they were getting worse by the day, she never knew where they were or when they were coming in, and it had to stop. Pa Bigsby backed her up.

'We live in a community and so we must abide by the rules. One of them is to be in time for meals. Otherwise, it is very inconsiderate to Ma.'

They apologised. Finally, Ma told them to sit down. They were lucky for she had kept them some shepherd's pie. No one was ever sent to bed without food in the *Pig* no matter how bad they'd been.

Afterwards, when they were clearing up in the kitchen alone and Ma had gone through to the bar to help Florrie, Elfie and Joe had a chance to have a proper talk.

They came to the conclusion that it was time to put the police in the picture. Elfie was still reluctant but Joe said that if Dimmock had set fire to the pawnbroker's shop and killed the Watsons there was no knowing what he might do next.

໑໑

They sat in the back room of the police station with Dowdy and Sergeant Feather and recounted their story, including their suspicions about the lawyer, Grimble.

'Glory be!' said Dowdy. 'And you've been keeping this to yourselves all this time? I don't know what Pa Bigsby'll have to say.'

Elfie had a pretty good idea. Missing supper would be nothing compared to this.

Sergeant Feather was tapping on his desk with a pencil and frowning. 'You realise these are very serious accusations that you are making against a member of the legal profession?'

'That's why we've waited to come and talk to you,' said Joe.

'Let's go through all this again then. You might write it down, Liam. Take a statement.'

Dowdy laid a pad of paper on the desk and dipped a pen into the inkwell.

'You think that this man Dimmock,' began Sergeant Feather, 'employed as a butler in the residence of Mr Clarendon-Smythe of Hampstead Heath, might have been involved in the kidnapping of the child Rosalind Trelawney?'

'We do,' Elfie responded at once.

'We have good reason to suspect he might,' added Joe. 'He visited the pawnshop on the Mile End Road earlier in the evening before the fire and said he would be back later.'

'To sort things out,' added Elfie.

'That could mean anything. It's scarcely enough to go on.'

'And then we saw him visiting Mr Grimble, the lawyer.'

'Yes, well . . .' Sergeant Feather leaned back in his chair and folded his arms. 'This is a sticking point. Do you seriously think we could bring him in for questioning? A lawyer? Without a shred of evidence against him.'

'He'd have our guts for garters,' said Dowdy, who had coined the phrase from Ma Bigsby.

'You're right there, Liam!'

'Are you not going to do anything?' cried Elfie. 'Let him get away with murder?'

'That house near Barnet,' said Joe. 'There's evidence in the attic that Rosalind was held there. We're sure of it.'

'Even if you're right about the handkerchief, it might have blown away by this time.'

'But it might not!' retorted Elfie. Sergeant Feather was infuriating. He needed a firecracker under him to get him to act. 'There's the ribbon under the mattress, too. That won't have blown away.'

'It's all a bit flimsy, if you want to know what I think.' The sergeant straightened himself up. 'But I suppose I could give a call to my colleagues in Barnet and ask them to go and take a look.'

'Why couldn't Dowdy go?' suggested Elfie. She wasn't sure Barnet bobbies would take much interest. 'Constable O'Dowd. It doesn't take long on the train. Joe and I could go with him and show him the way. The house is in the back-of-beyond. He could wander round for hours on end looking for it, getting nowhere. We could pay our own fares,' she added.

'Well, I don't know.'

'I've met Mrs Mallow.' Elfie was not going to let go and she could see that the sergeant was wavering. 'She's an elderly lady. She might confide in me more.'

'I suppose that's true.'

'It is! We got on really well together. She told me to come back another time.' Elfie decided against trying to explain that the elderly lady would call her Kitty. 'Well, if Mr Bigsby gives his permission –'

'I'm sure he will.'

Joe was not nearly so sure, and neither, in fact, was Elfie. They would have a lot of persuading to do.

☙☙

Later, Pa sat in his study chair, listening carefully, with his fingertips placed together, and at intervals he shook his head.

'We were never in any real danger,' Joe reassured him.

'I'm not so sure about that. The Watsons could have turned nasty if they'd caught you at this Willow Tree Cottage.'

'But they didn't,' said Elfie. 'Pa, Rosalind was kept in that room. Just think!'

'The police could investigate on their own, of course.' He steepled his fingers against his mouth, deep in thought.

Elfie and Joe could hardly breathe,

Then finally Pa came to a decision. 'Oh, very well! If Dowdy goes with you –'

'– we can't come to any harm,' finished Elfie.

Chapter Eighteen:
Back to Barnet

They took a train in the morning. Dowdy was pleased to be having a day out, a day away from Sergeant Feather.

When they arrived at Barnet station Dowdy engaged a horse-drawn trap. It was more robust than the one the Watsons had hired and the horse was younger. They bowled along the lanes and Dowdy commented, his arm dangling over the side of the trap, how pleasant it was to be in the countryside after the hubbub of the city.

'Perhaps I should try for a placement in the country. After Florrie and me are wed. We could get ourselves a nice little cottage.'

'Don't do that!' cried Elfie. 'You can't take Florrie away from us.'

Willow Tree Cottage looked exactly the same as before, as if nothing or no one had moved. Joe wondered, as they pulled up, if Maisie had heard about the fire at Mile End and the death of her nephew. It was possible that no one had informed her, for all the Watsons' possessions and papers would have gone up in the blaze.

'We shouldn't be too long,' Dowdy told the driver. 'A half-hour or so should do.'

The door opened before they had a chance to knock. Maisie looked startled when she saw a policeman standing there with Elfie and Joe. She half closed the door against them.

'Hello, Maisie.' Elfie held out her hand. 'Remember me? I called the other day.'

Maisie peered at her, then brightened. 'It's Kitty, isn't it,'

'Kitty?' queried Dowdy.

'Sometimes I use that name.' Elfie didn't meet his gaze but Dowdy didn't challenge it.

Maisie was staring at him. 'Has something happened? What do you want?'

'Can we come in?' asked Dowdy. 'I'm Constable Liam O'Dowd from the Stoke Newington police station in North London.'

'Stoke Newington? I don't understand.'

'If we might just come in? Easier to talk inside. More private.'

Not that there was anyone around to overhear anything.

Maisie hesitated, then reluctantly allowed them to enter. Dowdy took off his helmet and they followed her into the kitchen. Elfie noted with relief that the calendar was still hanging on the wall.

'I believe you have a nephew, Mrs Mallow,' began Dowdy, 'a Mr Stanley Watson, the proprietor of a pawnbroker's establishment in the Mile End Road in the East End of London?'

'A pawnbroker's? No, I don't think so. Not Stanley. He's in the garment business.'

'But your nephew is called Stanley Watson? And his wife's name is Beryl?

'Yes. What's happened to them?'

'Why don't you sit down, ma'am?' suggested Dowdy. Joe pulled up a chair. Still Maisie hesitated.

'Sit down, Maisie,' urged Elfie. 'Better if you do.'

The old lady took the advice and Elfie seated herself next to her.

Dowdy cleared his throat and gave a discreet cough behind his hand. 'I'm afraid I've got some bad news for you, Mrs Mallow.'

'Has something happened to Stanley?'

Dowdy told her about the fire and offered his condolences. She stared at him as if she didn't believe it.

'I'm very sorry, Mrs Mallow,' he repeated. 'I realise this must be a great shock for you.'

'Shall I make you cup of tea?' offered Elfie.

Maisie didn't reply. She looked as if her mind had gone elsewhere. Elfie got up and put the kettle on anyway. A cup of tea was Ma's remedy for everything.

Maisie took out a handkerchief and dabbed her eyes.

'Have you any other relatives?' asked Dowdy.

Maisie thought for a moment. 'There's my cousin

Madge in Nottingham. But I haven't seen her for some years.'

'Would she be available on the telephone? If not, we could arrange for you to speak to her at her local police station.'

'Drink your tea, Maisie,' said Elfie. 'It will help you to feel better.'

Maisie took a few sips.

'I'm afraid I have a few questions I must ask you, Mrs Mallow,' said Dowdy.

'What kind of questions?' Maisie sounded wary. 'I don't know anything about Stanley's business.'

'I believe, however, that Mr and Mrs Watson stayed here for a week about a month ago?' Dowdy took his notebook and pencil out of his top pocket.

'Who told you that?' Maisie was on her guard again. She eyed Elfie.

'The dates are marked on your calendar, aren't they?' Elfie jumped up and went to the wall to point them out.

'Let me take a look,' said Dowdy.

Elfie brought the calendar over to the table.

'Stanley wouldn't do anything wrong when he was here,' protested Maisie. 'He and Beryl just came to have a nice break in the country.'

'It wasn't very nice,' muttered Elfie.

'You don't deny, then, that they stayed here?' said Dowdy.

'I don't remember exactly.' Maisie's voice began to fade. 'It's my memory, Constable.'

There was nothing wrong with her memory when she'd last visited, thought Elfie. Had she known that Stanley was up to something? Elfie caught Joe's eye. He was thinking the same thing. Maisie was closing up like a clam.

'Did they bring anyone else with them?' asked Dowdy. 'When they came to stay?'

'Of course not. Who would they bring?'

'Mrs Mallow, we are investigating the kidnapping of a young girl.' Dowdy had on his best policeman's voice. 'It is a most serious offence so I would advise you to cooperate.'

'Kidnapping?' Maisie turned pale.

Dowdy stood up. 'Perhaps you might stay with Mrs Mallow, El . . . er, Kitty, while Joe and I investigate a couple of things upstairs.'

'You won't find anything up there,' said Maisie. 'I haven't been up in the attic for months. My knees . . .'

'We'll take a look anyway, if you don't mind.'

Maisie obviously did mind but was in no position to stop them.

'Come on, Joe lad. You can climb up to the skylight for me. You're more nimble than I am.'

Dowdy led the way out of the room and Joe followed.

'The skylight?' muttered Maisie.

'Don't worry, Maisie. They won't be causing any damage to your property.'

Elfie hated being left behind but someone had to stay with Maisie. Not that Maisie would be able to run off. Where could she go? Into the wood?

'This is all a terrible mistake,' cried Maisie. 'They shouldn't be allowed to snoop around my house like this.'

'He's a policeman investigating a crime.'

They listened to Joe and Dowdy's feet as they moved about overhead. Then they stopped. After a pause they heard the footsteps start up again. Now they were coming back down the stairs.

Constable O'Dowd entered the room, bearing a bright pink ribbon and an embroidered handkerchief. He held them up.

'We have just removed these two pieces of evidence from your attic room, Mrs Mallow.'

'I've never seen them before!'

'No, you probably have not. The handkerchief was stuck in the skylight window and the ribbon was lying under the mattress of the bed. Joe, here, is my witness.'

'I can confirm that,' said Joe gravely.

'They belong to the girl that was held in your attic,' said Dowdy.

'She's called Rosalind,' put in Elfie. 'She's only nine years old and she's my half-sister.'

'It had nothing to do with me!' cried Maisie.

'It had something to do with your nephew, though,' Joe pointed out.

'He's not my responsibility. Anyway, he's not my nephew.'

'He isn't?' said Elfie. This was the first she'd heard of it. What about that photo on the dresser? Although she supposed the child could be anyone.

'Who was he then?' demanded Dowdy.

Maisie shook her head. In a low voice she told them how Stanley and Beryl Watson had come to her door one day saying they were lost, and so she had invited them in.

'A foolish thing to do,' observed Dowdy. 'Especially the way it has turned out for you.'

'I was lonely. They were kind. Then they asked if they could store a few things in my attic from time to time. I never go up there – my knees . . . and once or twice they arranged to meet someone here. I never saw any of them. They always went upstairs. Said it was so they didn't get under my feet.'

'So you did all this out of the goodness of your heart?' asked Dowdy. 'Did they pay you?'

She nodded. 'The money came in useful.'

'You *must* have known they were up to no good,' said Elfie.

'I never asked any questions.'

'And then they booked a week at the seaside for you,' said Dowdy, 'and that left the way open for them to incarcerate a young girl in your attic.'

Maisie began to cry.

Crocodile tears, thought Elfie. To think she'd fallen for that nice old biddy act.

'I didn't know anything about a girl. I didn't do anything wrong. I was in Southend that week.'

'You aided and abetted a serious crime,' said Dowdy.

Maisy looked up at him, fearful. 'They won't put me in prison, will they?'

'That depends.' Dowdy took his notebook from his top pocket. 'I am now going to take a statement from you, Mrs Mallow.'

He asked detailed questions and recorded her answers in his notebook. Joe waited until Dowdy had finished, then added one further question.

'Mrs Mallow, did you ever see another man coming to the house with the Watsons, a big man, with broad shoulders, big hands, and a swollen nose?'

'Like a boxer's,' added Elfie.

'I'm not sure,' faltered Maisie.

'You've got nothing to lose now by telling us,' said Dowdy.

'I might have done. Just the once, though. And I only saw him through the window.'

'Was that before you went to Southend?'

Maisie nodded. 'I believe it was. A week or two. They went straight up the stairs. Same as usual.'

'Did you hear him say anything? It must have been difficult not to hear some of their conversations, surely?'

Maisie considered. 'He said something like, "That should fit the bill". I thought maybe he meant that the attic would be a good place for him to store something. Along with the other stuff Stanley left up there.'

'What did you think they were storing in your attic, Mrs Mallow?' asked Dowdy. 'Didn't it occur to you that they might be storing stolen goods of some kind in your home? You must have suspected that they were criminals?'

'I'd no idea, I swear I didn't.'

'You might have to swear to that in court.'

Maisie started to cry again. 'I was just glad of the company, and as I said, the money was handy. I'm on my own now . . .'

But Dowdy wasn't letting her put him off. 'So you are sure about the man Joe described to you?' he persisted. 'Could you identify him?'

'I don't know about that . . .'

'I bet you could, Maisie,' said Elfie. She turned to Joe, her eyes shining. 'It's Dimmock. It's got to be!'

Chapter Nineteen:
Closing In

'I'm afraid I must ask you to accompany us to the police station in Barnet, Mrs Mallow.'

Elfie was very impressed by the professional way Dowdy had conducted the interview.

'I haven't done anything wrong,' wailed Maisie.

'We are not saying you have but the fact remains that you did rent out your house to two people involved in a serious crime – the kidnapping of a young child.'

'But I didn't know. They didn't tell me. And I was in Southend.'

'You will be required to make a statement, however.'

'It's all right, Maisie,' said Elfie, no longer so annoyed with her now that she had been helpful. 'If you've done nothing wrong you've nothing to worry about.'

Still protesting her innocence, Maisie went out into the hall to fetch her coat. Elfie followed.

'Do you have your cousin's number? Madge, the

one in Nottingham?' asked Elfie. 'In case you want to phone her?'

'I suppose I might do.'

'She is on the phone then?' Elfie was curious about the cousin. The first time she'd visited, Maisie had told her she had no other living relatives. Perhaps it was so long since she'd seen Cousin Madge that she'd put her out of her mind.

'Oh yes,' said Maisie. 'Her husband is in business.'

Elfie wanted to ask what kind of business but thought the better of it. She was probably getting too suspicious. You had to be, though, didn't you, if you were trying to track down the truth?

'I'll just go and get it,' said Maisie. 'It's in my bedroom.'

The bedroom was off the hall. Maisie left the door ajar, and Elfie watched her through the gap. She just wanted to be sure that Maisie didn't try to nip out the back door even though reason told her that she wouldn't. Maisie went to a cupboard, took out a small notebook, and wrote something down. She tore out the page. When she'd replaced the notebook Elfie saw her lock the drawer and put the key into her handbag.

Dowdy and Joe were waiting by the front door.

'Ready then, ladies?' asked Dowdy.

They climbed aboard the trap and rode back to Barnet.

'Just as well the two ladies are lightweight,' observed the driver. 'Four's a bit much for Betsy to pull.'

Betsy trotted along at a leisurely pace. None of

them spoke. Maisie sniffed and patted her eyes with her handkerchief. She probably seldom left the house, thought Elfie. Except when she'd gone to Southend-on-Sea.

They were shown into a back room at the police station in Barnet. Dowdy and the sergeant-in-charge retired to discuss this turn of events. When they came back the sergeant took a statement from Maisie and when it seemed as if she might forget anything Elfie would prompt her.

'You can't lock me up, Sergeant.' Maisie kept shaking her head. 'I never even saw the girl.'

'We're not proposing to lock you up, Mrs Mallow. If you would just answer our questions we'll see you get home safely.'

'What if Dimmock comes back?' asked Elfie.

Maisie looked terrified by the prospect.

'I doubt he'll show his face again at the scene of the crime. He'd be foolish if he did.' Dowdy's voice was reassuring.

Elfie liked the sound of the phrase 'the scene of the crime'.

'But I'd advise you to keep your doors and windows bolted just to make sure, Mrs Mallow,' said Dowdy.

After she had given her statement Maisie asked if she could phone her cousin. The sergeant took her into another room to make a call.

'Poor woman,' said Dowdy, once she'd gone. 'Taken in like that by a bunch of crooks.'

'She did do it for money,' Joe reminded him.

'Hard up likely. That's what makes most people turn to crime.'

Joe nodded.

When Maisie returned Elfie asked if she'd managed to speak to Madge.

'I spoke to her husband. He said they'd try and come and visit me at the weekend.'

'Jolly good,' said Dowdy.

'And don't worry, Maisie,' Elfie told her again. 'Dimmock's in London. And like the sergeant said, he won't want to return to the scene of the crime.'

On the train back to London, Dowdy said, 'I expect Sergeant Feather will want to call in Scotland Yard.'

And he was right.

Inspector Barker arrived with a constable in double-quick time. There were two serious crimes involved, after all. The kidnapping of young Rosalind Trelawney and the arson attack in the Mile End Road.

Joe and Elfie knew the inspector from a previous occasion, when they had been investigating a conspiracy in the Chancery Lane office of Alfred Trelawney. Elfie had ended up in a doorway with a crook called Clinker holding a knife to her throat. That had been the time Joe had saved her by bowling a brick and hitting the man in the centre of his forehead.

'Wonderful shot that was, young man.' The inspector shook his head in admiration at the memory. 'I'll never forget it.'

'Neither will I,' said Elfie. 'I thought I was done for.'

Joe looked a little embarrassed. 'If we could just look at this case . . .'

'Yes, of course. Now then, tell me what you've been up to this time.'

They related their story again, with the inspector breaking in every now and then to ask a question or clarify a point. The constable scribbled like mad in his notebook.

When they reached the end, the inspector sat back in his chair. 'Well, well!' he exclaimed. 'You *have* been busy.'

'Rosalind's my sister,' Elfie reminded him.

'And one thing led to another,' said Joe.

'Indeed. That's how it often is. Or should be. But sometimes, in my line of work, we run up against a brick wall.'

That was just how Joe and Elfie had felt when they'd seen the headline in the newspaper about the fire in the Mile End Road.

Inspector Barker telephoned Scotland Yard and asked that two men be sent to the Clarendon-Smythe residence to bring in the butler Dimmock. He listened for a moment. 'You say Clarendon-Smythe is actually on the other phone at the moment? Good gracious. You'd better put him onto me.' While he listened, Joe and Elfie watched the inspector's expression changing. His lips were pursed now and he was frowning. 'I see,' he said slowly. 'When did this happen? About half an hour ago?'

'What's happened?' cried Elfie, thinking about Rosalind.

Dowdy hushed her, since Inspector Barker was still on the phone and trying to listen.

'Whereabouts exactly?' he was asking. 'Tell your manservant to touch nothing. I'll send my men round straightaway and I shall call on you myself very shortly.' He replaced the receiver and turned back to face the company. 'Mr Dimmock was found in an alleyway about half an hour ago. He's been shot.'

Elfie shrieked.

'Blimey!' said Sergeant Feather. 'That's a turn up for the book. Just when we were onto him.'

'Quite a coincidence,' observed Inspector Barker.

'Who found him, sir?' asked Dowdy.

'A member of the public. A passer-by. He recognised Dimmock and called at the house. Mr Clarendon-Smythe sent his young manservant round to identify him.'

'That'll be Quirk,' said Elfie.

'I'd better get over there now myself.' Inspector Barker put on his hat. 'I'll be in touch, Sergeant Feather. And thank you for your help, Joe and Elfie,' he added with a smile.

He left straightaway with his constable.

'Mr Clarendon-Smythe won't be at all pleased,' said Elfie. 'Losing his butler.'

'He might be upset that the man's dead,' suggested Sergeant Feather.

'Not him,' scoffed Elfie. 'He's an Ogre. He ain't got a heart.'

'*Hasn't*,' murmured Joe.

'Perhaps it's time you two went home,' said Dowdy. 'Ma and Pa Bigsby will be up the wall wondering where you are.'

'You'll let us know if you hear anything, won't you?' asked Joe.

'Don't worry, we'll keep you informed.'

'Promise, Dowdy?' said Elfie.

'I promise. Now away you go, before we have Pa Bigsby round here looking for you.'

They set off at once for the *Pig and Whistle*.

'We've lost our main suspect now,' said Elfie, who was getting into the way of talking like the police herself.

'But worse than that,' rejoined Joe, 'is that there must be someone else involved.'

'The person who shot Dimmock?'

'Somebody did. But how could they have known the police were onto him?'

They considered that for a moment.

'You don't think it could have been Greasy Grimble?' suggested Elfie.

'I can't see him shooting someone in a back alley.'

'But he could have got someone to do it for him.' Elfie knew that there were often hit men hanging out around the docks. They would do a job for a few quid.

'If Grimble thought Dimmock would grass on him,

he might have decided to get rid of him,' said Joe. 'If, of course, he was involved. We don't really know that.'

'I'll bet he was.'

'But we need evidence, Elfie. Maybe we should pay him a visit,' said Joe.

'What about Ma and Pa?'

'I don't think we should waste any time.'

Elfie was surprised – Joe was usually so cautious. He raked in his pockets for coins and checked he had enough. He did. Stepping out into the street he flagged down a cab. He really was throwing caution to the winds, thought Elfie. Not like Joe at all.

Chapter Twenty:
Confronting Grimble

The traffic was so thick that the cab was forced to go at walking pace much of the time. Joe kept taking out his watch.

'You bothered?' asked Elfie.

'I've just got a funny feeling about Grimble. I mean, if he did kill Dimmock . . .'

'You mean he might scarper,' said Elfie.

Just as they pulled up at Grimble's office the door opened and out came the man himself. He was not dressed in his lawyer's clothes. He was wearing a long grey coat and a grey bowler, and he was carrying a large portmanteau.

Joe and Elfie leapt out of the cab. He stopped dead when he saw them.

'Hey!' the cabbie called down from his perch. 'I want my fare.'

'You pay him, Elfie,' said Joe, handing her some money.

Joe turned to confront the lawyer. 'We'd like a word with you, Mr Grimble.'

'Who do you think you are? Scum!' Grimble swung his bag at Joe but Joe had no problem in side-stepping it. 'Get out of my way!'

The cab took off and Elfie joined Joe.

'We want to talk to you about Dimmock, Mr Grimble,' said Joe, moving a little closer to the lawyer.

'Do you indeed?'

'Did you know he'd been shot?' put in Elfie.

'No, I did not. And I know nothing whatsoever about it, if it is true.'

'It is.'

'Move aside at once! I've got a train to catch.'

'I don't think you should go anywhere, Mr Grimble,' said Joe, 'not until the police have had a chance to talk to you.'

'And I think you should mind your own business.'

Grimble put his hand into his overcoat pocket and a second later was holding a small black pistol to Joe's forehead. 'You've gone too far this time, boy. I would like you to come back into the office with me.'

'Don't go, Joe,' cried Elfie.

'He has no choice, I'm afraid. Not unless he wants a bullet in his brains. You too, miss.' Grimble gestured with his free hand towards the door. Grimble kicked it open behind him, keeping the gun steady. 'Go in slowly, the two of you, and don't try any of your monkey tricks. If you make a false move I won't hesitate to pull the trigger and our friend here will end up as a corpse.' His voice was calm, cold.

For once, Elfie was too petrified to speak. She remembered Clinker holding the knife to her throat and how Joe had rescued her. Now it was her turn. But how? She wasn't any good at cricket. There was no way she could throw a rock and hit Grimble in the forehead. She took a quick glance along the street. It was deserted.

'Do as I tell you,' ordered Grimble. 'Now!'

They edged inside the empty office, as instructed. The lawyer shoved the door shut with his elbow, never taking his eye off Joe.

Elfie scanned the room, looking for inspiration. Surely there was something here she could use? A clean blotting pad sat on the otherwise empty desk. It looked as if Grimble had been clearing up. There was virtually nothing lying around except for a big typewriter on another desk. A Standard. She had to do *something*! Joe was standing to attention, not even blinking, while Grimble continued to hold the gun to his head.

Grimble would never let either of them go. He had too much to lose, and it seemed he'd been about to skedaddle. *Think!* Elfie told herself.

'What's that? There at the window?' she cried.

In the brief moment that Grimble was distracted Joe brought his arm up and knocked the pistol flying across the room with Elfie diving after it. She grabbed it. Meanwhile, Joe managed to get a stranglehold round Grimble's neck. He was taller and much stronger than the lawyer. Grimble gurgled and struggled but Joe held him fast.

'Put that down, Elfie,' shouted Joe, 'before you shoot yourself in the foot. And phone the police.'

'Don't you dare touch that telephone!' croaked Grimble.

Joe released his hold on the man's neck a little but continued to struggle with him. Elfie went to the receiver on the wall, lifted it and asked the operator to put her through to Stoke Newington police station.

'Quickly! It's a matter of life and death. There's a man here with a gun.'

The operator took her at her word.

'Is that you, Dowdy? Listen, it's Elfie here. We're in Grimble's office. Yes, Grimble the lawyer. He was about to shoot Joe but Joe's holding him down on the floor so you'd better get here quickly.' She paused for breath.

'Slow down, will you?' said Dowdy at the other end of the line. 'What in the name of goodness are you talking about? What's all this about Mr Grimble and a gun?'

'He was going to shoot us!'

'Is this one of your jokes, Elfie?'

'No, it's true! Cross my heart and hope to die.'

Dowdy was silent for a moment. Elfie could imagine him scratching his head.

'Dowdy,' she yelled. 'Can you hear me? I'm dead serious. You've got to get here and bring Sergeant Feather with you. We think Grimble killed Dimmock.'

'Utter lies,' cried Grimble in the background.

'Elfie, do you really know what you're talking about?' asked Dowdy.

'Of course I do! You've got to believe me! You don't want the killer to get away, do you?'

'All right, hang on, we'll be there as soon as we can. But you and Joe had better be right or you'll be in deep trouble with Sergeant Feather.' Dowdy hung up.

'They're on their way. The police,' added Elfie to bring the point home to Grimble.

'Elfie,' said Joe, 'look in the bag and see if you can find something we could tie him up with. A belt or some string, maybe.'

'Take your hands off my bag,' yelled Grimble. Joe had slackened his grip a little, worried he might choke the man. 'You'll be sorry for this,' Grimble went on. 'You can't prove a thing.'

'We'll see about that,' returned Joe. 'You've got a gun for a start,'

'And I have a licence for it.'

'You might well have,' said Elfie, 'but you were holding it to Joe's head.'

'In self-defence.' Grimble continued to struggle. He landed a kick on Joe's shin.

Elfie had opened the bag and was rummaging through it, chucking clothes in all directions. Finally she pulled out a bit of what looked like a dressing-gown cord. She held it up.

'This do?'

'Fine. Bring it over.'

Joe hauled Grimble into a chair and pulled his hands behind his back.

'You'll pay for this, the two of you, I'm warning you!'

'Try and tie the cord round his arms, Elfie,' said Joe. Beads of sweat stood out on his forehead.

Between them they eventually managed to tie Grimble securely.

'There's a white silk evening scarf in the bag too,' said Elfie. 'Maybe we could gag him with that?'

'I don't think that'll be necessary,' said Joe. 'He's got no one –' He broke off. 'I think somebody's coming.'

They raised their heads. It sounded as if some kind of conveyance had drawn up outside and now there were voices shouting. Somebody banged on the door and Elfie ran to open it. In came Dowdy, closely followed by Sergeant Feather and two other constables.

Grimble addressed Sergeant Feather. 'Untie me at once. These two hooligans broke in and tried to rob me. And then they had the nerve to tie me up. They were about to gag me! This is outrageous. I fully intend to lay charges against them.'

'We'll untie you, Mr Grimble,' said Sergeant Feather reasonably, beginning to do so, 'but we will have to ask you a few questions. Young Elfie here, whom we know very well, is no hooligan. Neither is Joe. They have made serious allegations against you.'

'Rubbish!'

'I'm afraid we will require you to come to the station and make a statement.'

Grimble, once released, stood up, smoothed back his hair and straightened his coat. He faced the sergeant. 'And I will have very serious allegations to make against them.'

'You will be free to do so.'

'There's his gun.' Elfie pushed it across the floor with her toe and Dowdy picked it up.

'I have a licence for that gun,' said Grimble. 'I took it out in self-defence when they broke into my premises.'

'There doesn't seem any sign of a break-in,' commented Dowdy, looking around.

The door opened again and in came Inspector Barker with two more constables. He surveyed the scene in the office.

'Mr Grimble was going to shoot Joe,' Elfie informed him before the lawyer could say a word. 'We know he was thick as thieves with Dimmock. He'd even have shot him to shut him up. And we think he might have helped to kidnap Rosalind. In fact, we're pretty sure he did, Inspector.'

'She *thinks*,' said Grimble scornfully. 'That won't stand up in a court of law, you know that, Inspector. Besides, I had absolutely nothing to do with the kidnapping of Rosalind Trelawney, except that I assisted Mr Clarendon-Smythe in paying the ransom to the kidnappers. I have been Mr Clarendon-Smythe's lawyer for more than twenty years and he will vouch for my good character.'

'Good character, huh!' snorted Elfie. 'Wait till he finds out you've been double-crossing him.'

Grimble merely smiled.

He's so sure of himself, thought Elfie. *So smarmy.* But of course even she realised that the lawyer was right. They had no hard evidence to prove that he had killed anybody. At least, nothing that would stand up in court.

Dowdy was examining the gun.

'Is it loaded?' asked the inspector.

'Yes,' Dowdy sniffed. 'But it hasn't been fired today.'

'Are you sure?' cried Elfie.

Dowdy nodded.

'I told you so,' said Grimble. 'I did not kill Mr Dimmock. I have been in my office all day. My clerk can testify to that. He was here until half an hour ago.'

'He could have got someone else to do it, Inspector,' said Elfie. 'He was about to scarper. Look, there's his bag!' Suddenly she felt less sure of herself.

'I was about to go over to Paris for a few days,' said Grimble. 'And now I have missed my train. Inspector, I wish to charge these two for breaking and entering my premises with a view to robbery. Also, for restraining me and holding me captive against my will. I demand that you arrest them forthwith.'

Chapter Twenty One:
Arrested

Elfie and Joe sat in a small room in Scotland Yard with Elfie's father and Pa Bigsby. They were waiting to hear if Grimble was going to go ahead and press charges. In other circumstances Elfie would have been thrilled to get inside Scotland Yard. But not today. Neither her father nor Pa Bigsby had been at all pleased to hear what they had been up to.

'It's all a pack of lies, Papa,' said Elfie. 'We weren't trying to rob him. We just wanted to stop him running away.'

'I believe you, love,' said her father. 'So does Pa Bigsby, I'm sure.'

'Indeed I do. Dowdy and Sergeant Feather found what you told them to be very convincing. And Inspector Barker does as well, though he has to try to remain impartial. But you know that you should not have gone there on your own.' Pa Bigsby suddenly sounded very severe.

'You most certainly should not have done,' agreed Mr Trelawney. 'It was an invitation to trouble. I've already lost one daughter . . .' Elfie's father squeezed her hand.

'We're sorry we've worried you,' said Joe, 'but I had a feeling that Grimble might be about to take off.'

'And he was,' pointed out Elfie. 'So what else could we do?'

'As you know, he claims that he was merely going to Paris for a few days holiday,' said Mr Trelawney. 'There is nothing incriminating in that.'

'But he might not have come back,' protested Elfie.

Her father was looking worried and she, like Joe, did feel sorry about that, for he was troubled enough. But they had done it all in the cause of trying to track down Rosalind's kidnappers. Her father and Pa Bigsby had both been amazed when they'd told them what they had discovered about Willow Tree Cottage, the Watsons and Dimmock.

'This woman, Maisie Mallow, was she sure that it was Dimmock that she'd seen?' asked Mr Trelawney.

'Her description sounded very like Dimmock,' said Joe.

'You know that is not convincing enough.'

'I do, but the fact that he was shot afterwards was suspicious, do you not think so, sir?'

'That is puzzling, Joe, I admit. So all your suspects appear to be dead now?'

'*Somebody* shot Dimmock,' Joe reminded him.

'So the assassin must be alive,' came in Elfie. 'He

could have been another member of the gang. And we think that person is Greasy Grimble. Don't we, Joe?'

'He doesn't strike me as a gang member. But I suppose he might have employed the Watsons and Dimmock.'

'That's what we think!'

'But you can't prove it.'

'No. Not yet,' said Elfie.

'Elfie,' said Pa Bigsby sternly, 'I do not want you and Joe to become involved in this matter any further. The police will take over now. I am sure your father will agree upon that.'

'Absolutely. You could have come to serious harm. You more or less did!'

The door opened to admit Dowdy.

'Mr Grimble has decided to drop the charges,' he announced.

'Good!' declared Pa Bigsby, rising to his feet.

'It is good, but it is also interesting that he has decided so,' mused Mr Trelawney. 'It could be because he doesn't want to muddy the waters any further. Otherwise, I think he would have wanted his pound of flesh. He is that kind of man.'

'You mean he'd be afraid that something might come out to incriminate him?' said Joe. 'So it was easier for him to let the whole thing drop?'

Alfred Trelawney nodded.

'He might slink off to Paris now,' cried Elfie. Surely he wasn't going to get away as easily as that!

'Inspector Barker has requested that he stay in

London in the meantime to be available for questioning with regards to your allegations,' said Dowdy, sounding unusually pompous.

'So the inspector must have doubts himself,' said Mr Trelawney as they left to call a cab. Dowdy had said he would call in at the *Pig* on his way back.

Riding back to the *Pig and Whistle*, Elfie was thinking about Maisie Mallow, and, as was her custom, she had to express her thoughts out loud.

'Do you know, when I visited Maisie Mallow the first time she told me she didn't have any other relatives except for her nephew Stanley.'

'And he wasn't even her nephew,' Joe reminded her.

'But the second time she said she had a cousin in Nottingham.'

'I see what you're getting at,' said Joe. 'Does she really have a cousin in Nottingham?'

'That's what I was wondering.'

'If she doesn't, then who was she phoning?'

Alfred Trelawney broke in. 'Do you think she might have been more involved than she made out?'

'It's possible,' answered Joe. 'I wonder, could her call be traced? She made it from Barnet police station. The operator might remember.'

'It would be worth a try,' said Alfred Trelawney. 'They can't have so many calls in a day. We'll ask Constable O'Dowd when he comes back.'

'Oh, just call him Dowdy, Papa,' said Elfie. 'Everybody else does.'

Ma greeted them with open arms but listened with horror when she heard the whole story.

'May the Lord save us! You'll be stopping my heart one of these days, the two of you, the things you get up to. You could have got yourself killed, Joe.'

'But he didn't,' said Elfie.

'Elfie saved me,' Joe grinned.

'But it was you who wrestled Grimble to the ground.'

'Don't tell me anything more.' Ma laid a hand on her heart. 'Come and have some dinner. You must be fair starved. You, too, Alfred. I persuaded your dear wife to eat with us earlier.'

Clarissa was sitting in an armchair in the corner of the kitchen. She had wept when she'd heard about Rosalind's handkerchief and the pink silk ribbon. 'My poor child. She must have been feeling desperate.'

'Expect she still is,' said Elfie. 'We've got to get her out of there.'

'But how?'

'If we could prove that Grimble diddled her grandfather that might soften his heart.'

'You'd never do that,' said Clarissa sadly.

Elfie turned to Joe. 'I wonder if Grimble could have had the money stashed in his portmanteau?'

'Wouldn't you have found that, with all that rummaging around you did? If he did he'll have moved it by now. It would be wise of him if he had.'

'He's a lawyer, after all,' said Alfred Trelawney.

Dowdy arrived while they were eating and was persuaded to join them. Elfie hoped he wouldn't go into the bar to sweet-talk Florrie afterwards. She was dying for him to go back to the station and phone Barnet.

He did go in to chat to Florrie, but not for long, and left soon afterwards on his bicycle, saying he'd do his best. He would come back as soon as he had any news.

Elfie couldn't settle. She wandered about the house, venturing even into the public bar though she was chased out quickly by Florrie. They were not allowed in the bar except for the sing-songs on Saturday evenings. Joe was in Pa's study, playing chess with him. The Trelawneys had stayed in the kitchen with Ma.

Elfie went out onto the pavement where she could watch for Dowdy's return.

Mad Meg came down the street singing *Nellie Dean*, one of Ma's songs. Meg knew most of the words though the tune was off-key.

'*There's an old mill by the stream*
Nellie Dean!
Where we used to sit and dream –'

Mad Meg broke off. 'What are you doing out here, young Elfie?'

'Waiting for Dowdy?'

'He's Florrie's sweetheart.'

'I know that.'

'Is Joe your sweetheart?'

'He's my friend.'

196

Mad Meg wasn't truly mad but she could be very annoying at times.

'Aren't you going in to see your brother?' asked Elfie. Sad Sid was already in the bar.

Then Elfie spied Dowdy and rushed towards him.

'He's Florrie's sweetheart,' Mad Meg shouted after her.

'Did you get the number, Dowdy?' asked Elfie breathlessly.

'I did indeed. I have it here.' He took a piece of paper out of his top pocket. 'Let's go inside. We'd best go up to Pa's study.'

Dowdy laid the paper on Pa's desk.

'We checked. It is the telephone number of Mr Grimble's office.'

Chapter Twenty Two: Running Off

'We told you so!' cried Elfie. 'Maisie must have rung to tip him off!'

'We've asked the Barnet police to bring Mrs Mallow in for questioning.'

Dowdy said he would return in the morning to keep them informed.

Elfie could hardly bear it. A whole night to get through while they waited! In spite of that, she dropped off to sleep immediately. It had been a full and somewhat tiring day.

Joe, though, wakened early, a little after dawn had broken. There was still a rosy light in the sky above the rooftops. He got up and decided to walk over to the police station. The street cleaners were out with their brooms and a few carts clattered by.

Dowdy was drinking tea from a large mug and yawning. There hadn't been much going on, apart from a break-in at the sweet shop. A couple of lads. The nightwatchman had seen them. They'd taken a jar of striped balls and one of jelly babies. There had been no cash in the till. Mrs O'Grady was too fly to leave any there overnight.

'Any news from Barnet?' asked Joe.

'Not yet. They said they'd get back to me this morning.'

Joe joined Dowdy in a cup of tea and while they were drinking the telephoned shrilled.

Dowdy answered. 'Hello, yes, it is PC O'Dowd here.' He whistled. 'So she's done a runner, has she?'

Joe looked up. Surely they hadn't lost yet another of the accomplices! They were fast disappearing, one after the other, in one way or another.

'So you think she took off in a hurry?' asked Dowdy. 'She didn't take time to clear the place out? Well, well! Not such a sweet little old lady after all. I've met a few of those in my time. Let me know if you get any leads.' He hung up.

'What now?' said Joe.

'You tell me. Funny case this is.'

'I'd better get home or else Ma'll think *I've* done a runner!'

He sprinted all the way.

Elfie was setting the table while Ma stirred the porridge. Pa had his monocle in place and was reading the morning paper.

'You were out early the day, Joe,' remarked Ma.

'Went over to see if Dowdy had any news.'

'And did he?' asked Elfie.

'Maisie Mallow has disappeared.'

Elfie dropped a plate. It split into two neat halves.

'Honest to goodness!' exploded Ma. 'Keep your mind on what you're doing. We're not made of money.'

'Sorry,' said Elfie meekly. 'I couldn't help it. It was just with Joe telling me about Maisie . . .'

Pa folded his newspaper. 'You know you are not supposed to be involving yourselves in that business any more. Leave it to the police. It's their job.'

'They wouldn't have got this far without us,' rejoined Elfie.

'And how far is that?' said Ma. 'Three folk dead and now one appears to have scarpered.'

'There's still Grimble,' said Elfie.

Pa shook his head.

The rest of the children came crowding in.

Ivy noticed the broken plate. 'Has she broke another one?'

'*Broken*,' said Elfie. 'And yes, I have.'

'I'm docking her pocket money,' put in Ma.

Ivy grinned and Elfie made a face at her behind Ma's back, but unfortunately not Pa Bigsby's. He reproved her with a glance.

After breakfast, Elfie walked with Joe to the bus stop.

'No further now,' Pa had warned. 'Your studies are suffering, Elfie. Your mind is too often elsewhere.'

In the queue while they were waiting Elfie had a sudden thought.

'You remember when Maisie went into the bedroom to get her cousin's phone number? She took a notebook out of a drawer, wrote a number on a piece of paper and locked the drawer again afterwards.'

'Leaving the notebook inside?'

Elfie nodded. 'She just took a piece of paper with her. And if she took off in such a hurry –'

'She might have left the notebook behind.' Joe glanced up the street. 'Here's the 39 coming. I'll see you this afternoon.'

After the horses had pulled away from the stop Elfie stayed where she was, thinking about that notebook. Then she took off like an arrow, heading towards the police station.

Dowdy was still in the station, still yawning. Sergeant Feather had been summoned to Scotland Yard and the other constable had had to go to a road accident.

'Dowdy,' Elfie began straightaway, 'could you phone the Barnet police again?' She explained about the notebook. 'Ask them if they could go back to the house and see if it's still there.'

Dowdy rolled his eyes, but he dialled and spoke to the policeman on duty in Barnet.

'They'll go and take a look as soon as they can,' Dowdy assured Elfie. 'Now you'd better hoof it back to the *Pig* or Pa'll be cross with you.'

But Pa was already cross. He told Elfie to remain after school and write an essay entitled *The Consideration of Others*.

'But –' she started to say, and got no further. Pa was not listening.

Elfie was desperate to go down to the office after school and meet Joe. It was so hard to concentrate. They were studying the reign of Queen Victoria, from the beginning to the end. Elfie could only think of her as a stout, fierce-looking elderly lady in a white cap.

The consideration of others! She could write about Rosalind, she supposed. She and Joe had been considering her for weeks now. She'd seldom been out of their heads. It was strange, though, that for all she thought about her sister, Elfie couldn't quite remember what Rosalind looked like. Not properly. She hoped she would see her soon.

'Where did Queen Victoria like to spend her summer holidays, Elfie?' asked Pa.

Elfie thought it might be the Scottish Highlands. Her mum, who had died when she was born, had come from Scotland.

'Balmoral,' shouted Ivy.

'I knew that,' said Elfie fiercely. 'He didn't ask you.'

Their tiff was cut off by a tap on the door and the arrival of Ma.

'I've got Dowdy downstairs. He's very anxious to speak to Elfie. You, too, Pa.'

'Very well,' said Pa, rising from his chair. 'Read your books until I return, children. And no noise, please. Books should be read peacefully. And, Mabel, you might take the little ones to the playroom and read to them from Robert Louis Stevenson's *A Child's Garden of Verses*.'

Elfie raced downstairs ahead of Pa. Dowdy was sitting in the kitchen with Florrie, having a cup of tea.

'Did they find it?' cried Elfie.

'Find what?' asked Ma.

'Maisie Mallow's notebook.'

'They did indeed.' Dowdy unbuttoned his top pocket and took out his notebook. 'I noted down a list of the numbers. There were no names opposite them, just letters or symbols.'

'She must have wanted to keep them secret.' Elfie felt sure they were onto something important now.

'Shall we sit down?' suggested Pa. 'It would be easier for us to peruse the list.'

'I'll leave you to it,' said Florrie. 'I've the brasses to do.' And off she went with her long earrings birling. Elfie had never seen her without them. She wondered if she wore them in bed.

Elfie sat at the table squeezed between Pa and Dowdy. There were more than a dozen numbers on the list. Maisie must have known more people than Elfie thought. She'd seemed so solitary, sitting in Willow Tree Cottage all alone.

'Recognise any of the numbers, Dowdy?' Pa put on his monocle.

'Not specifically. But I did notice there was a Hampstead one.'

'And?' Elfie held her breath.

'It's the phone number of the Clarendon-Smythe house and look – it has the letters D, G and Q written beside it.'

Chapter Twenty Three:
The Letters G, D and Q

'I thought G might be Grimble,' said Dowdy. 'And D could be Dimmock. Then there's Q. I suppose Q could be a question mark?'

'It's *Quirk*!' yelled Elfie. 'He's the top manservant. Lizzie didn't like him. She said he was a nasty piece of work and she always thought he was hand-in-glove with Dimmock.'

'I'll have to report all this to Inspector Barker.' Dowdy stood up and put on his helmet. 'I daresay he'll want to go over to Hampstead himself.'

Elfie followed Dowdy outside. 'Ask him if Joe and I could come too,' she pleaded. 'We know all about Maisie Mallow. We can give evidence and we wouldn't get in the way.'

'I doubt if the inspector will go for that,' said Dowdy, taking off on his bicycle.

Elfie went back into the house.

There was no time to return to lessons. Ma was already banging the lunch gong. Elfie sat beside Florrie at the table and, for once, Florrie talked about her wedding to Dowdy. She was excited. It wasn't long now.

They were going to rent two rooms in a house near the park, she said, a living room and a bedroom, with shared kitchen and bathroom.

'We've worked out that we can afford it, with Liam's wage going up to twenty-five shillings and sixpence a week, along with the rent allowance of one and sixpence. And I'll be keeping my work on at the bar.'

'Dowdy might get to be a sergeant one of these days,' said Elfie.

Florrie had bought her outfit, a two-piece, oyster-coloured silk suit and a wide plate hat to match, decorated with pink roses.

'We'll have to think what you girls are going to wear.' And then Florrie sighed. 'I still can't imagine having the wedding without Rosalind. It don't seem right.'

'You never know.' Elfie kept her voice down, so that Ivy couldn't overhear. 'We might have Rosalind back with us by then.'

'Liam doesn't seem too hopeful. He says that no matter what happens that horrible grandfather of hers is never going to let her go.'

'A miracle could happen. He might slip on some potato skins and fall downstairs on his head.'

They giggled together. There had not been too much laughter of late at the *Pig and Whistle*. Clarissa arrived as they were clearing away the lunch things and Ma poured a cup of tea straightaway.

The door opened and in came Joe and Alfred Trelawney, surprising them.

'I heard from Inspector Barker that he was planning a visit to the Clarendon-Smythe house, to question the manservant,' Elfie's father explained.

'Good!' said Elfie.

'Some lunch, Alfred?' invited Ma.

'I've no time, thanks, Ma. I'm going out to Hampstead myself to see what's going on.'

'Oh, Alfred,' cried Clarissa, 'what if you should see Rosalind . . .' She held her breath.

'I doubt they'll let you in, Alfred,' said Pa. 'Best not raise your hopes too far.'

'I expect not but I have to go. Joe will accompany me.'

'And me!' Elfie sprang up. 'Please, Papa!'

'Come quickly then!'

When they reached Hampstead, Alfred Trelawney asked the cabbie to drop them off a little way short of the Clarendon-Smythe house.

They were about to turn into the back lane when they caught sight of the police wagon drawing near. There seemed to be a number of men aboard.

They hurried round the alley to the back gate, which was bolted from inside, as before. They could hear the sound of men's voices coming from the front of the house. The police must have arrived and perhaps, even now, they would be ringing the bell and demanding to be admitted.

'Old Clarendon-Smythe won't half throw a fit,' said Elfie gleefully.

'Hush,' cautioned her father.

Footsteps were heading towards them. Someone was in a hurry.

'Stand to the side,' said Mr Trelawney.

The bolt was pulled at the back of the gate and out came Quirk at the double. Joe stuck out his foot and caught the man under the knees, sending him flying across the lane to land on his face with a yell of fury. Joe was on top of him in a flash, though Quirk looked in no condition to fight him off. He'd been badly winded and blood was pouring from his temple.

'Have you killed him?' cried Elfie.

'Of course not.'

Her father produced a white handkerchief, which Joe pressed on the man's forehead. Two portly constables came puffing round the corner.

'What's going on 'ere?'

'There is the man you are looking for.' Alfred Trelawney pointed to Quirk.

'You're sure, sir?'

'Dead sure.' Elfie answered for her father. 'He's called Quirk.'

'That's him then.' The constables hauled the manservant to his feet and dragged him round the corner.

'Look. The gate's still open.' Elfie gave it a little push.

They slipped inside and Joe closed the gate behind them. The back door of the house also stood open.

'Should we go in?' asked Joe.

Alfred Trelawney nodded. There was no one about but they could hear loud voices coming from a room at the front of the house. Glancing up, Elfie saw two maids standing at the top of the stairs, bent over the bannisters, listening. That dragon, Mrs Dimmock mustn't be around any longer to keep an eye on them. Elfie gave the girls a little wave.

They moved up the hall towards the front room.

'What are you doing here, Mr Trelawney?' Dowdy was standing on guard at the entrance and he was obviously alarmed to see the new arrivals. 'The inspector won't be pleased.'

'That can't be helped.'

'You can't go in!'

'We don't intend to.'

A pity, thought Elfie, but at least they could listen in, for the voices in the room were ringing out clearly, and the door had been left a few inches ajar. Deliberately, perhaps, in case Dowdy was needed. Squinting through the gap Joe made out the tall, haughty figure of Mr Clarendon-Smythe while, close by, sitting in an armchair, reclined Greasy Grimble, with his legs crossed, looking quite relaxed. Shifting his position, Joe saw Inspector Barker, on his feet, flanked by two constables.

'This is totally outrageous!' Mr Clarendon-Smythe

was furious. 'How dare you enter my house in such a manner with a posse of constables! I will not let this pass, Inspector. I am a personal friend of your commander.'

'The nature of my business might indeed be called outrageous, sir,' replied Inspector Barker. 'I am investigating several extremely serious crimes. Three murders, as well as the kidnapping of your own granddaughter.'

'I know nothing whatsoever about any murders. As for the kidnapping of my granddaughter, what is it that you have to say to me on that matter? Have you apprehended the culprit?'

'Not exactly.'

'Not exactly!' Mr Clarendon-Smythe's tone was openly contemptuous now. 'What then?'

'We now know where she was kept during her captivity and we also know who owned the house.'

'Is that so?' Mr Clarendon-Smythe moderated his tone.

'Rosalind was incarcerated in a cottage outside Barnet belonging to a woman by the name of Maisie Mallow. Your granddaughter was held hostage there by a couple called Stanley and Beryl Watson.'

'Have you arrested them then?'

'Unfortunately not. They died in a fire in their pawnbroker's shop in the Mile End Road in London.'

'So you were too late to charge them?' Mr Clarendon-Smythe gave a dry laugh.

'We have evidence, though, that Rosalind was held in the attic of that cottage.'

'Evidence? Of what nature?'

'Two articles belonging to Rosalind were found there.'

'A pity, then, is it not, that this Watson couple was not apprehended earlier?'

'It would have been an advantage, certainly,' agreed the inspector.

Looking round, Elfie saw that the two maids had now crept down to the bottom of the stairs.

'So what else do you have to report to me?' demanded Mr Clarendon-Smythe impatiently. 'If there is nothing, I suggest you leave.'

'We believe that Mr Dimmock, your late butler, committed the arson attacks at the pawnbroker's shop where Mr and Mrs Watson died.'

'You *believe*?' sneered Mr Clarendon-Smythe.

'All this evidence is totally insubstantial,' said Grimble, uncrossing his legs and speaking for the first time. Elfie was surprised that he should be in the house at this time.

Inspector Barker continued, 'Mrs Maisie Mallow, the owner of Willow Tree Cottage, made a statement to the police in Barnet, confirming that the Watsons had used the attic during the week she was away. We also know now that she made a telephone call to warn some person that the police would be looking for Mr Dimmock.'

'All very interesting.' said Mr Clarendon-Smythe, 'but you have yet to convince me that you have any definite proof of anything.'

'We have traced Mrs Mallow's call.'

Joe noticed Grimble sit up straighter.

'Mr Clarendon-Smythe,' the inspector carried on, 'the number that Mrs Mallow telephoned was that of Mr Grimble's office.'

Grimble was on his feet now. 'I deny receiving any telephone call from this woman Willow, or whatever she was supposed to be called.'

'Mallow.' The inspector remained calm.

'Half of those operators are far from intelligent and their command of English is poor.'

One of the two maids was now advancing along the hall. She reached the group at the door. Dowdy frowned but did nothing to turn her away.

'We believe,' Inspector Barker went on, 'that the recipient of the call then telephoned someone and asked him to . . . take care of Mr Dimmock.' He chose his words carefully.

'Preposterous!' Mr Clarendon-Smythe's face had turned an angry red. 'Are you claiming that my lawyer Mr Grimble would be involved in such matters? Please leave now! Nothing you have told me can be substantiated.'

'I am not so sure.'

Outside in the hall, the maid tapped Dowdy on the arm. 'I know about that call. I took it,' she whispered.

'Go in, then,' said Alfred Trelawney, 'and tell the inspector what you know. What is your name?'

'Mary, sir.'

Dowdy pushed the door open wider and ushered the girl into the room.

'What is she doing here?' Mr Clarendon-Smythe exploded.

'Mary has evidence to give, sir,' Dowdy told the inspector.

'Very well. Speak then, girl.'

Mary swallowed hard. 'I took a call from Mr Grimble on the day Mr Dimmock was found murdered.'

'Mr Grimble telephones here often,' interrupted Mr Clarendon-Smythe. 'He is my lawyer, after all.'

'I know that, sir. But he asked for Mr Quirk. Not you.' There was a pause.

'Are you absolutely certain it was the same day?' asked the inspector.

'Certain sure, sir. The next day was my day off, you see, and I was looking forward to it.'

'Did you hear anything of the telephone call?'

'That girl is a liar, Inspector,' interrupted Mr Clarendon-Smythe. 'You can't trust her. My wife has caught her stealing.'

'I never stole nothing, Inspector.' Mary looked more surprised than offended.

'Carry on, Mary, and tell me what you overheard.'

'Mr Quirk said he would go and see to it straightaway. He then went upstairs and Dolly saw him go into his room and open a drawer. He had a gun in that drawer.'

'How do you know that?'

She looked nervously at her employer, then turned back to the inspector. 'We've seen it. We was in there cleaning one day and he'd forgotten to lock the drawer.'

'You see what kind of girl she is!' snapped Mr Clarendon-Smythe. 'Snooping around the house. Opening other people's drawers.' He swivelled round and pointed to the watchers in the doorway. 'I should have guessed you'd be snooping around somewhere. Get out of here at once, Trelawney! And take your two friends with you! This is my house. I'll have no riff raff here!'

But he was cut off by the inspector. 'I will conduct this interview, if you don't mind, Mr Clarendon-Smythe.'

'I do mind.'

Inspector Barker ignored him. 'Constable O'Dowd, go out and ask the men to bring Quirk in here.'

Elfie was keeping a close eye on Grimble. He was looking queasy, as well he might! She hoped he didn't have that little black gun in his pocket though surely he wouldn't be so stupid as to try to escape with all these police around?

Dowdy came back with Quirk, who was what Ma Bigsby would call a 'sorry-looking sight'. His shirt was torn and his forehead bloody.

The inspector addressed him. 'We have some questions to put to you.'

'Don't know nothing,' muttered Quirk.

'You received a call from Mr Grimble on the fourth of June. You then went to your room and took a gun out of your drawer and left the house. I put it to you that you went in search of Mr Dimmock, found him in an alleyway, and there did shoot him through the head.'

Elfie pressed her hand to her mouth.

'You don't have to answer,' Grimble put in quickly.

The inspector turned his attention to him. 'Mr Grimble, did you or did you not telephone to this house and ask the maid to fetch Mr Quirk?'

'I did not! That girl is concocting a story. For what reason I can only surmise. Perhaps she took a notion for this young man and he rejected her. Now she is seeking revenge. You know what young girls are like!'

The inspector swung back to the manservant and looked him straight in the eye. 'I put it to you again, Mr Quirk, that you killed Mr Dimmock on the instructions of Mr Grimble?'

Quirk glanced away. 'So maybe I did. But it was the lawyer who put me up to it.'

'You mean Mr Grimble? This gentleman here, present in this room?'

'Yes, sir.'

'That is slander!' Grimble was spitting with rage.

Mr Clarendon-Smythe stepped in. 'It most certainly is. I can vouch for my lawyer's good character and his integrity in all matters and know others of importance in society who will support me in this.'

The inspector turned his back on Mr Clarendon-Smythe. 'Mr Quirk, for what purpose have you been associating with Mr Grimble?'

'Number of things,' muttered Quirk.

'Illegal things?'

'Suppose so. The Watsons were in on it too, them

215

from the pawnbroker's in the Mile End Road. But I never fired their shop, honest I didn't.'

'Do you know who did?'

'Might have been Dimmock.'

'*Might have been*,' mocked Mr Clarendon-Smythe. 'The man doesn't even know his own mind.'

The inspector pressed on. 'Were you involved in the kidnapping of young Rosalind Trelawney, Mr Quirk?'

'Only a bit.'

'What did you do?'

'Delivered the letters to Mr Trelawney.'

'The ransom notes?'

'Say no more, Quirk,' cried Grimble. 'It will be in your best interest to remain silent.'

'Please be quiet,' said Inspector Barker wearily. 'Mr Quirk, was Mr Grimble involved?'

'I collected the letters from his office.'

Joe suddenly sprang forward. 'The Standard typewriter!' he exclaimed. 'We saw one in his office, didn't we, Elfie? If you examine it, Inspector, I think you will find that the letter "n" is worn. That's where those ransom notes must have been written.'

The room was still.

'We will require you to come to the station, Mr Grimble,' said Inspector Barker. 'And you, too, of course, Mr Quirk.'

Grimble, who had been studying the carpet at his feet, looked up. 'Inspector,' he said, 'I was not the prime mover in this. I refuse to carry all the blame.'

'So, tell us, Mr Grimble! If not you, who was the prime mover?'

Grimble took a deep breath and said, 'Mr Clarendon-Smythe.'

Chapter Twenty Four: A Wedding

Elfie cried out. All eyes were on the upright, commanding figure of Mr Clarendon-Smythe.

'Beats me. Why would he would want to kidnap his own granddaughter?' Dowdy was shaking his head.

'To get control of her. That man wants to control everything.' Alfred Trelawney strode across the room and confronted his father-in-law. 'Isn't that right, Clarendon-Smythe? It was a devious plan you hatched. To steal your granddaughter and then offer to pay the ransom. With special conditions attached, of course.' His voice was bitter.

'I wished to raise her in the traditions of *my* family.' Mr Clarendon-Smythe had lost none of his haughtiness, even at the moment of his ruin. 'Not yours, Trelawney. There is bad blood in yours.'

'Bad blood!' spluttered Elfie. She put her hands on her hips. 'Just because his granny came from Bermuda and had brown skin. What a nerve! What about you? You're bad to the bone! You *stole* my sister.'

'Yes, all right, Elfie,' said her father, putting a hand on her shoulder.

'*She* is another reason.' Mr Clarendon-Smythe looked down his long nose at Elfie. 'And *him*.' It was Joe's turn. 'Your so-called apprentice.'

'And an excellent one he is, too. It is due to the efforts of Joe and Elfie that we have finally arrived at the truth.' Alfred Trelawney looked Clarissa's father in the eye, perhaps for the first time ever. 'It is the most despicable thing I can imagine, a man putting his own flesh and blood through such an ordeal. You are beneath contempt, Clarendon-Smythe.'

'Hear, hear,' murmured Joe.

'May you rot,' added Elfie with relish.

'You will certainly rot in prison, at the very least,' said the inspector, who had stood back to allow Alfred Trelawney to have his say. 'Murder and kidnapping are capital crimes.'

'Rosalind!' cried Elfie suddenly forgetting her anger.

'Yes, Rosalind,' said her father. 'Let us go and find her at once.' He turned to Mary. 'Can you take us there?'

'Certainly, sir.'

'And we shall take care of these three,' said Inspector Barker. 'Mr Quirk, Mr Grimble, and Mr Clarendon-Smythe. Handcuff them, men.'

Elfie and her father raced out of the room and up the stairs behind Mary.

A woman's voice called out, 'Mary, is that you?'

Mary came to a halt. 'Yes, Mrs Clarendon-Smythe.'

'Come at once!'

'She's in the drawing room,' whispered Mary. 'I have to attend to her.'

'Take us in,' said Alfred Trelawney.

Mrs Clarendon-Smythe was reclining on a chaise longue. But she sat up straight when she saw Alfred Trelawney and Elfie.

'What are *you* people doing here? What's going on? All that shouting and banging of doors.'

'Your husband has been arrested for the kidnapping of his granddaughter,' Alfred Trelawney told her, 'and as an accessory to murder.'

Mrs Clarendon-Smythe's eyes glinted with anger. 'Impossible!'

She knows, thought Elfie. *She's going to pretend that she doesn't but she does.*

'We need the key to the attic,' said Mary. 'Please.'

'My daughter is locked in the attic. So, where is the key?' demanded Alfred Trelawney. He held out a hand.

Mrs Clarendon-Smythe sank back and raised a limp hand. 'In that cupboard. Mary, bring me my smelling salts.'

Mary ignored that request. Swiftly she retrieved the key and they ran up the next two flights of stairs.

'That's it there.' Mary stood to the side.

Alfred Trelawney unlocked the door.

Sitting on the windowsill, a book open on her lap,

her long fair hair drawn back with a ribbon, her face pale as milk, was Rosalind, looking like a princess in a fairytale.

'Papa!' she cried. 'Elfie!'

๛

The celebrations at the *Pig and Whistle* were in full force. Florrie looked radiant in the oyster-coloured silk suit and her long pearl earrings. Dowdy's smile stretched from ear to ear as he twirled his new wife round to the strains of *Daisy Bell*, played by Frankie on the harmonium. Sad Sid conducted and Mad Meg sang along with the rest, on a slightly higher note, while the company swayed in time with the music.

'*Daisy, Daisy,*
Give me your answer do!
I'm half crazy,
All for the love of you . . .'

Florrie had already given Dowdy her answer. They had been married that morning. There were six bridesmaids: Elfie, Ivy, Mabel, Nancy, Dora and little Vicky. And Rosalind. They wore an array of pink, blue and lilac organdie dresses and carried bunches of sweet peas. Dowdy's brother Owen had come over from Ireland to be best man and had taken a fancy to Lizzie, who had been invited to the party. Joe was an usher in a pale grey suit, a gift from Rosalind and Elfie's father.

Alfred Trelawney was dancing with his wife Clarissa, who, after so many weeks of misery, was smiling.

Joe was partnering Elfie, as would be expected. They were arguing from time to time about which way to turn, as would also be expected.

'I wonder what's happened to Maisie Mallow?' said Elfie.

'Perhaps we shall never know,' said Joe. 'What does it matter?'

Even Ma and Pa Bigsby had taken to the floor.

'On such a special occasion as this,' said Pa, 'it is necessary for everyone to participate.'

The song went on.

'It won't be a stylish marriage,
I can't afford a carriage,
But you'll look sweet upon the seat
Of a bicycle made for two!'

The strains of the music reached out into the street and up to the sign hanging high above the pub door. The pig, too, was smiling, while he danced and played along on his whistle.

About the Author

Joan Lingard has had published more than thirty books for children and thirteen for adults. *Tom and the Tree House* won the Scottish Arts Council Children's Book Award. *Tug of War* was shortlisted for the Carnegie Medal, the Federation of Children's Book Groups Award, the Lancashire Children's Book Club of the Year, and the Sheffield Book Award. *The Guilty Party* was also shortlisted for the Federation of Children's Book Groups Award. *The Eleventh Orphan*, the book that introduced Elfie to thousands of readers, was shortlisted for The Royal Mail Children's Book Award and the UK Literary Association Children's Book Award 2010.

Joan was awarded the M.B.E. in 1998. She is married with three children and five grandchildren.

The Eleventh Orphan

Mr and Mrs Bigsby of the *Pig and Whistle*
in Stoke Newington already look after ten
children. When Constable O'Dowd brings
them an eleventh orphan he found on the
streets Ma Bigsby is reluctant to take her.

But there's something about Elfie, it's the
first day of a new century and Ma loves a mystery.
Just why does Elfie possess a little watercolour
of the *Pig and Whistle*?

As the mystery unfolds, Elfie's world will
change completely.

SHORTLISTED FOR:
THE ROYAL MAIL CHILDREN'S BOOK AWARD
UKLA CHILDREN'S BOOK AWARD
WEST SUSSEX CHILDREN'S BOOK AWARD
THE LANCASHIRE SCHOOL LIBRARIES AWARD